FOREWORD

When Evil Came To Stay continues the 21st Testing Protocol. The first books was actually a NanoWriMo project from 2018.

I don't usually go off on a tangent or whim, but the original book in the series, Cyborg: Redux was built around the premise that at some point in the future, people won't be able to help themselves with cloning technologies, cybernetic implants and so on. Perhaps there was also a healthy dose of Borg (Star Trek) thinking went into the storyline as well.

What if these implants can and are able to be generated by a human body?

The children then took on their own very large and scary personas. Those who will work on infiltrating and so on. Honestly, if I didn't know better, I'd say my brain is a scary place to hang out!

Back to the matter at hand though. There is one more book in the series after this. It's the culmination of years of work and I hope you enjoy it...

Remember if you do enjoy it to leave a review in any location of your choice - and if not, do let me know why.

FOREWORD

Imogene Nix
2021

This book was written during NanoWriMo 2019 (Cyborg: Redux came in 2018 and Children of a Greater Evil in early 2019) It's taken time to get it ready for publication but I'm so pleased to see this series coming to an end.

Erin and David's story has been building through the series and had to be told because they have been supremely patient.

So has my husband, the awesome Mr Nix. His patience regularly allows me the scope to investigate fight scenes, cloning and so much more. My browser history is at best eclectic! YouTube has a lot of information as well (just in case you're looking for information yourself.)

To my Mother In Law, June. Cause she reads and shares my books... Her indefatigable support is welcome. Every day.

Thanks also to my team. Charlotte, Michelle, Suzi, Keri, Sassie and more. Without you, this would be a much harder road to tread on my lonesome.

Imogene Nix
2021

WHEN EVIL CAME TO STAY

21st Testing Protocol

Imogene Nix

Love Books
Publishing

Print ISBN 978-0-6484841-7-2

CHAPTER ONE

*E*rin McNally slumped into the seat and rubbed the ache from the still healing injuries she'd gained guarding Senator Daniella Villede. Weariness blanketed her, and her eyes drooped. The van wasn't the best place to hunker down for a nap, but it was all she had. Well, that and her surveillance partner, Franklin Mann.

Mann was a bear of a man, strong and capable. Reliable. A good friend.

"Settle in. I'll let you know if anything worthwhile happens." His voice flowed over her, and she nodded, hunched a little further down in the seat, and tugged the ball cap over her eyes.

Drowsiness washed in and out, darkness wrapping itself around her, and she fell into the bottomless well…

She pulled the car to a stop outside a secured entrance at the side of the building. Checking front and left, there was no sign of combatants. "We should be good."

Erin tugged the car door open and had just moved to the other side, opened the door for the senator, and started to usher her to the door of the building when the wail of the security klaxon filled the air. Jesus fucking Christ!

Erin stopped midstride, noting dimly that the senator did too. Now she pushed her, snatching at the door and shoving the woman inside. "Get back!"

She shoved the senator and pulled the door shut before the woman could regain her composure and argue the toss. Right now, Erin's job was to ensure her safety.

In the seconds after she jerked the door shut her hand felt down to the snap on her pistol. Before she could draw it fire streaked through her body, and she jerked, her eyes wide as a loud 'oomph' echoed along with the sounds of screaming.

It wasn't her. It couldn't be her.

Her knees turned to water as the senator screamed and battered at the door. "No! No! McNally!"

Her hand reached to her stomach. Wet. Hit. Shit!

Erin jerked awake, her hand once more rising to her stomach. Heart rate pounding so blood rushed and adrenaline spiked.

"It's okay, McNally. We all have nightmares."

Her head whipped to the side, and she caught the harsh planes of Franklin staring at her. "You need to talk to someone though. Before you can't cope with it. You know the drill."

She grunted, hoping to head him off before he said any more. Preferring instead to bury those memories and thoughts deep within her psyche. She'd deal with them when she was damn well ready. Sure as shit, that wasn't now. *Tell yourself that, Erin, but you know this is getting harder to ignore.*

Erin rubbed her aching brow surreptitiously, hoping Mann wouldn't see it. "Any movement?" She wriggled in the seat, then repositioned the cap on her head.

"A few children. Threat level minimal with no significant movement at this time." Erin exhaled. Surveillance required patience, something she was chronically short of at the best of times. She squinted through the plexiglass of the vehicle and sighed when all she could see was a distant mass.

"Hand me the spyglass and I'll see what's going on," she said. "Just in case they're just beyond our view."

They'd decided to borrow a pair of old-fashioned, non-electronic spyglasses from the display case in the interrogation unit, given there was no way it could be picked up on sensors after learning their technological surveillance units could and had been compromised during the operation to shut down the maturational facility.

Franklin passed over the surprisingly heavy brass tubed unit, and she stretched it out and looked into the distance.

"Wow, it's surprising just how much we can see with this."

"Really? I mean, it's got no graphical enhancers or…" His words died off as she glanced in his direction then peered once more down the tube.

"Maybe that's part of what we need to do. Employ some old-fashioned techniques that they can't hack."

She reached up and scratched the back of her head, considering her own words. It might just give them a competitive edge.

She hunched down and scanned. "There. I'm seeing about thirty or so. Huddled together, in the entrance to an alley just beyond the far entrance." She watched for a moment, seeing the chatter and hands pointing in their direction. "I'd say the surveillance has made us, and this job is done. Let's get out of here and report."

"You're sure?" Franklin spoke quietly as she collapsed the object in her hands.

"Yeah. Besides, I want to make a couple of suggestions to the senator and Jonah."

He shrugged, started the vehicle, and pulled away. "Any specific route?"

"Yes." It took a few seconds for her to formulate a plan and another to realize he'd no doubt argue with her decision. "Straight ahead, toward the children."

"What?" he bellowed, and Erin winced.

"Just trust me. Drive slow and steady. I want a look at that alley, so turn on the outer cameras. There's no need to be covert now."

He grunted but carried out her instructions, and she reached out and dragged up the miniature viewing unit attached to the dash of the vehicle. This way she could watch as they drove past and wouldn't interfere with the video acquisition. Even better, if their vision was jammed, she'd still have the information to report back.

A mass of children waited in the alley as she'd suspected, and at the back was a door, open…

For an instant, the urge rose to tell Franklin to stop. To let her zoom in and maybe see what was inside, but reality raised its head, and she sighed. All that would do was place herself and Franklin in danger. As it was, she was taking a risk driving past the throng of child-warriors. She had firsthand experience of just how dangerous they were.

Once past, Franklin sped up and took the most direct route back to the base. It wasn't as if anything they were doing wouldn't have already been watched. She'd seen one girl reach up and touch the side of the vehicle as it slowly slid by the crowd.

Just before the entrance to the base, she spoke again. "Franklin, pull over. I need to check something."

She grabbed her pack, riffled around inside and drew out the scanner, then opened the door and headed for the driver's side of the vehicle.

It wasn't easy to see initially, blended white, the same color as the vehicle, but just beside the driver's door sat a small tracker unit. The tiny, button-sized item was flat enough that it almost resembled a sticker, but it glowed slightly.

Mann climbed from the driver's side of the van. "What is it?"

With care, Erin squatted down and placed the scanner over the item, waiting as it hummed. "It's a new generation stealth tracker. Bounces back both visual and verbal, but contains no known compounds that would lead me to believe it's dangerous." She slid her fingernail below the surface and peeled it off, grimacing as it also stripped the paint from the car.

Erin dropped the tracker to the ground then stomped down hard and followed up with grinding it under the heel of her boot.

A quick glance assured her it wouldn't be usable, nor had any of it stuck to the heavy rubber sole of her footwear. "Let's get back to the base."

The car rocked as Franklin climbed within. "Well..."

"There's one thing we've learned—they're learning. We'll need our wits about us if we have any hope of defeating them. Come on."

D avid grunted as his sister, Senator Daniella Villede, now the most senior member of the government, shoved a folder of papers into his hands.

His lips curled in dismay. "Why me?"

"Because you're my brother. An agent with an illustrious history, and the people here on the base trust you. That along with the fact that you've just returned from a mission, and I don't have anyone else to spare to the task."

He seethed. "Placing infants is the job of—"

Daniella groaned. "Look, I know this isn't what you expected. We didn't plan to find maturational chambers. We didn't realize we'd return with dozens of babies in need of families." Her eyes widened. "*Trust me*, we were and are totally unprepared for this situation. I need someone I can count on to sort out the initial placements, to ensure the families are prepared for what's to come. We don't know how fast these babies will mature, and they will need all sorts of care we have no information on that's specific to their needs. I don't have time to arrange it, and neither does Jonah. McNally is out on location with Franklin, Clarissa and Michael are involved in the medical and psych assessments... There is no one else we can trust to do justice to this task, David."

He grunted and accepted the sheaf of papers. "Just the initial placements. Right?" He flicked through them, finding photos beside a short description of health and physical attributes. "LV? LM? What are they?" He glanced up into his sister's narrowed gaze and a trickle of disquiet twitched down his spine.

"Those are the designations... According to LV-1, or Liv as she wants to be known now, that was their names. It's apparently based on the parental names, hence they're designated two letters. The numbers are the number of child they are in the process. LV-1 means she was the first child of those parents. The adoptive parents will need to come up with new and suitable names for the children once they're placed."

Each file page was numbered, and by the end he'd reached twenty-four. "How the hell…" He sighed and shook his head. The inhumanity of what they were facing was a dart to his psyche. "Fine, do we have candidates?"

"Yes. Lots. All from the base. We're going to initially only make these children available to long-term couples who've been assessed as secure at this time. Down the track, if more become available, and once the political and social situation stabilizes, we'll take applications from the wider public."

Daniella swiped her hand over her face, and for a moment, David read the concern she seemed to be trying to hide. "Is there a process in place for meeting with and considering the applicants?"

"They'll be presenting to the medical facility in the morning. Meet with them and gauge how well you think they'll cope with special needs children, which is how we're currently viewing them. Clarissa will be there to assist you and to explain the finer points of their immediate physical and maturational needs. I will need you to match the children to the families you think can cope, and it has to be quick. We don't have a lot of time right now, David. We're in the middle of a war, and caring for them in the infirmary isn't going to work if there's an incursion on the base."

Her words didn't fill him with any form of confidence as he left the office and headed for the medical facility with the sheaf of papers tucked under his arm.

I'm an agent, not a bloody child welfare services officer. "What the hell would I know about kids?" But for all that, he understood why Daniella and Jonah needed someone capable of sizing people up quickly.

The sound of an approaching vehicle captured his attention, and he looked up in time to see the white van containing Franklin and Agent Erin McNally pull up to the facility. He strode up to the vehicle and scanned her face as the two agents climbed from the car.

Inside his belly, the jitter that had taken up residence there since she'd been injured raised up and smacked him hard. "Agent McNally? Everything all right?"

It took every ounce of willpower to control the outburst that really wanted to erupt. *Are you injured?*

McNally stared at him, her eyes wide, the dark chocolate of them beckoning, just as they always did. "I'm, uhhh... Everything's good. When did you get back?"

A ruddy glow washed over her cheeks, entrancing him, then disappeared as her hand moved to her waist.

"You're sure you're well enough to be on active duty?" he asked.

"Oh yeah. They cleared me for light duties. Nothing too strenuous. I've been surveilling..."

Franklin hovered at her side then sighed, shook his head, and broke the uncomfortable air surrounding them. He muttered something that sounded suspiciously like 'get it together' before wandering off.

"What are you doing?" she asked David.

He held up the folder, waving it. "Placing children." He couldn't quite control the disgust in his voice, and she chuckled.

"Never thought I'd see the day. Come on. I wanted to check in on them, I've got a vested interest these days."

He turned and pinned her with his gaze. "What do you mean?"

"I was in on the mission when they were found. The facility? It was huge, and it had this air of... I don't know, it sounds silly, but it was cold and evil, and I'm being fanciful." She shrugged. "Come on, I know where they are. Besides, it gives me an opportunity to update you on what I saw today."

David trailed behind her, ignoring the sway of her hips and the scent of her that wound around and stole the oxygen from his lungs. He'd already made too many mistakes with this woman, and he was fairly sure she'd refuse anything more to do with him on any kind of emotional level.

"And what did you see today?" he asked.

"Massing kids. At the abandoned school. Not doing much and no sense of urgency at this point. They did try tracking our vehicle, but I found the chip and destroyed it."

That gave him a moment of disquiet, but right now, it was better to know where they were and that they weren't actively preparing for an attack. *Small mercies.*

The door to the infirmary swung open with a squeak, and the faint antiseptic tinge filled the air, tickling his nose, while the sound of his feet on the white tiles squeaked. Without stopping, she moved to the left-hand side corridor and strode along, clearly confident in her direction.

At the far door, she stopped and signaled to the sanitizer dispenser. "Important to sanitize. The babies haven't received any form of vaccinations, and we're still not sure how susceptible they'll be to illnesses."

He nodded, amazed at how much she already knew about the babies.

Once she was satisfied they were adequately prepared, Erin opened the door and they stepped into a room featuring twelve white cots. Babies cooed, arms waving, and he watched McNally advance to the first, bend over, and touch the cheek of one of the two babies resting within.

"They're due for a feed, so grab one each and head over here." His sister-in-law, Clarissa, lounged in an armchair, cradling one of the babies, directing the nipple of a bottle filled with white liquid—milk, his brain told him—to the mouth of the rooting baby.

McNally reached down and picked one up then surprised David by placing it in his arms. "I'm not..."

"Well, now you are. Clarissa will have the bottles already made up. Take a seat next to her while I grab this little one."

He stared at her. "Really, I wouldn't know where to start."

"We all started that way. Come on, David. Given Daniella

contacted me and informed me of how we're going to spend the next week, it won't hurt you to get up close and personal with these bundles of cuteness." Clarissa hugged the wriggling baby closer and nudged a bottle toward him. David watched Clarissa, startled at the way she just seemed to sink into the seat and handle the baby.

McNally, cradling the other baby from the crib, nudged him, and he gave a defeated sigh and headed in the direction of his sister-in-law.

The night drew in, and Erin slumped to the bed, exhausted as she usually was at the end of her day. Her side ached, and she knew pushing herself wasn't the best choice, but what other was there?

"I refuse to not do my best to sort this mess out." Except this mess was greater than anyone had expected when they'd first met Clarissa. She'd known about Michael, having been in the same professional circles as David. She shied away from thinking about him. That led only to more misery, and even worse, the blooming of need.

She'd had enough of that in her life already. *Emotion free.* If only it were so simple to ignore the burning hunger inside her.

When the senator—Daniella, as she'd be told to call her—had created the team at President Yin's command, it hadn't seemed so totally overwhelming at the beginning. All they'd been required to do was find out who was undertaking illegal Cyborg therapy. It was only once they'd started digging more and more that the evil plan had surfaced.

Erin rose, tugging off the wrinkled shirt, and smelled it, her nose crinkling at the stink. One of the little darlings had done rather more than just burp on her. Erin balled it up and threw it into the corner with all the other camouflage print clothing. "I'd better attend to them tonight."

Reaching the bathroom and turning on the water, she exhaled and looked down. The scar was still angry-looking, puckered and raised.

Maybe she should go see Michael and let him take a look. He'd be able to tell her if this was normal a couple of weeks after the wounding.

Stepping into the shower, she released a sigh, letting the water sluice over her skin. Erin cleared her mind so all that remained was the pleasure as her muscles relaxed under the tingling spray of the water. She stayed there for several minutes, calm and relaxed, before turning it off and stepping back into the steam-filled room, reaching blindly for a towel.

The knocking on the door to her room began, and she wrapped the large cotton bath sheet around herself, tucking in the edges before calling out, "I'm coming."

She hurried to open the door a crack to see David standing there, his eyes shadowed.

"Can I come in?" he asked.

She stared at him, her mind mush.

"May I?"

"Oh. Just a moment, I need to…" Her hands fluttered as she groped for control of the situation, overwhelmed with his proximity and her lack of clothing. He followed her in.

She slammed the door shut, narrowed her eyes, and shook her head. *Standing here foggy-brained won't deal with whatever he wants to see you about.* Now Erin scurried, tugging open the single door wardrobe and peering within. One last uniform.

Erin retreated to the bathroom, clothes in hand. "Just a moment," she called breathlessly. With quick moves, she dropped her towel into a wet pile on the floor, then grabbed the underwear she'd found in the bottom of the cupboard and tugged them on. She grabbed the shirt and shoved it over her head before reaching for the pants and stepping into them.

"Everything all right?" David's voice filtered through the door.

She forced herself to inhale deeply before heading back to the room's door. She carefully opened it, and his gaze narrowed.

"I didn't mean to intrude." His gaze wandered past her to the pile of clothing on her floor.

"I was just showering. So, what can I do for you, sir?" Tagging on the last word she hoped would be enough to make him realize there was no connection between them, nothing more than a mistake in the heat of emotion.

"I wanted to talk to you about that night, Erin. I…" He reached out, and she flinched back.

"I don't think so. Everything that needed to be said was. I had a nightmare, you woke me, and things happened that shouldn't have. Is that all?" She raised an eyebrow, well aware that would goad him into action. She needed David gone so she could find her center once more.

"Erin, dammit, we need to talk. Come for a coffee with me. *Please.*" The word contained so much emotion, and heaven knew Erin wanted to go with him, but it wouldn't be wise, her rational mind screamed.

"No, sir. Now, if there's nothing else?" She strode to the door, opened it, and gripped on like it was a lifeline and willed him to leave.

Defeat filled his face. "Okay, for now. But we do need to talk about this. About us. We're not done, Erin. Not by a long shot." He turned and marched past her.

Erin watched him go, knowing damn well if he decided to push it, they'd be revisiting this conversation again before long.

She closed the door and backed up into the room before slumping back on the narrow bed. So, unlike the one… *Stop it! Don't remember!*

If only it were so easy to turn off her memories.

She woke, arms holding her against a hard chest. The half-light from the bathroom the only illumination.

"I've got you, Erin." David's voice betrayed the depth of emotion, rough and dark like liquid chocolate.

She shivered, her body still frigid from the nightmare. "Please, don't leave me." Her fingers dug into his shoulders, clinging to him. Holding him so close and absorbing the reassurance.

"I won't. I'll be right here. Always here for you." His breath whispered over her hair, ruffling it, while his hand moved in tender circles over her back.

Her nerves jumped and danced at his proximity. Some of it was left over from the nightmare of the shooting, but the rest was a reaction to the tenderness of the caress.

Tears burned in her eyes, scalding her cheeks, wetting his bare torso.

"Erin?" His fingers stilled, dragging her closer.

Awareness flared and she tugged away.

"Stay still, Erin. Just there." He exerted careful pressure, so that once more her face rested against his collarbone. Just a tiny shift and her lips would be in contact with the warm, muscled skin.

An odd yearning rose.

Erin moved, her lips opening over the flesh. Tasting the saltiness of his flesh.

He shuddered in response. "Erin."

His hand cupped the back of her head, curling into her hair and guiding her gaze upward so she could read the ardor in his eyes.

"I want to kiss you, Erin."

A long second passed, dragging her into a well of pleasure and hunger. When their lips touched, her whole body ignited, fire licking at her, and their mouths crushed, opened, and the heated cavern of his mouth beckoned.

The interest between them, long denied, flared into light in a second. His tongue danced against hers, while need bubbled and boiled in her gut and her most secret recesses melted with arousal.

He groaned, or she did. Her mind unable to grasp who gave voice to the furious sensations battering her mind.

Her arms wound around his neck as he reached for her breasts, diving under the loose nightshirt.

She moved and fire streaked, roaring pain searing her mind, and she tugged away on a screech of agony.

"Oh, Erin! I'm sorry. Let me..."

Tears soaked her cheeks again as she cautiously cupped her side, and she fought for control of her breathing and stomach. The echoes of pain had her gut threatening to release itself then and there.

"Please. Get me a pain pill and some water." Her voice sounded scratchy as she closed her eyes, refusing to watch the real-life, god-like

man in the bedroom with her move to the side. Her hand came away damp, and she opened her eyes, glancing down.

Blood. Great, she'd likely opened the wound. When David returned, he passed her the glass, and without thinking, she reached out with the blood-crusted hand.

"Damn!" He knelt at the edge of the large bed and reached for her shirt, but she brushed his hand away.

"It's not bad. If you'd grab me a washcloth, I'll sort it out."

He growled. "I caused it, I'll clean it up." Fury at himself echoed in his words, and she shook her head.

"No. It's not a lot, and I can and will clean it up. Seriously. Please, just go."

He stilled, frozen, and his eyes snapped to her gaze.

"Please."

He hooded his gaze, the green fire dimming. "I'll leave you this time. But we're not done, Erin."

She bit her lip as he moved to the bathroom, grabbing what she'd need, then left without a word.

Erin sighed. "Just one more mistake in a lifetime of them."

She carefully shucked her outer clothes and settled into the bed in her underwear.

Morning would come all too quickly, and she needed to rest.

CHAPTER TWO

*D*avid cradled the drink in his hands. It wasn't how he'd intended to spend the evening.

Michael joined him at the table, his gaze locked on the finger of alcohol in David's glass. "Everything okay?"

"No," David growled. "Erin is refusing to talk to me." He gulped the fiery liquid down and reached for the glass of water in the center of the table.

"Ahh." Michael raised his hand and beckoned to the server who scurried in his direction. "I'll have an iced tea. No sugar, just mint."

"Of course, sir."

"It's funny sitting here with you, and you're drinking tea instead of scotch." David snorted and took another sip of his drink, savoring the burn in his throat.

"By product of this." He raised his hand, and David caught sight of the crisscrossing of surgical scarring on his brother's skin.

"So much has changed. You and Daniella are both married." He shrugged, unsure how to ask his brother for advice. After all, he'd always been the more capable with women. When had that changed?

"Want to share what's on your mind?" Michael murmured.

David waited as the waiter returned and placed the mint tea in front of Michael and asked David if he'd like another drink.

"Yeah. Then I'm joining the tea brigade."

The waiter glanced at him quizzically then shrugged.

"I fucked up, Mike. I mean, after the accident, when she was at my house, I made a move. Messed it up big time, and now she refuses to talk anything but work. Before this, she was my friend and colleague. It's gone." The emptiness inside him spooked him. What if there was no way to get her back as a friend? *Have I really scared her off forever?*

He drained the glass of water in his hand and carefully placed it on the faux-wood tabletop. Waiting for the pearls of wisdom.

Michael remained silent, and the seconds dragged out. The server returned and replaced David's empty glass with a filled one, the amber liquid glowing in the muted lighting.

"Mike?"

"Look, David, I don't know your Erin very well. She strikes me as a woman who is focused on her career. One who has a very clear sense of duty. Very contained in her emotions. You're telling me you've messed up, so I think you're going to have to gain her trust, if indeed you've shattered it. But I suck at reading women."

Michael didn't smile at him, and David sighed. No easy answers, he guessed. "You have it together with Clarissa."

"She's different. For some reason, with her I don't need to second-guess, because what works comes naturally. You need to find that equilibrium with Erin, otherwise, just maybe, she's not the right woman for you."

"Huh, fat lot of sense that makes." David snorted and took a sip from the glass. "But Clarissa is great. The one that's kind of odd is Jonah and Daniella. I mean, who would have thought..."

The two brothers laughed, knowing exactly what hadn't been said.

Jonah and Daniella. Two very different people, yet somehow it appeared that they'd found their happily ever after together.

Their sister was poised and powerful, polished and stepping up to assume command of the government. Jonah, strong also. Powerful too but without the polish, but ready to put his life and future on the line to protect the woman he loved. A career army man, though also one hell of a strategist.

In silence, both brothers drained their glasses, then Michael made to rise but pinned David with a piercing look. "Heard you were visiting the infants today, which is great. We need to change their names as a priority. They're maturing quickly, and it's a first step in giving them a future. We need to rehome them, and the quicker the better for everyone."

David grunted. "I'm thinking of telling the adoptive parents, once they're placed, to use their letters to create names. I begin interviews tomorrow with the prospectives. There's twenty-four infants so..."

"Twenty-three." Michael spoke quietly, and David sighed.

"I'm sorry." He genuinely was. Michael had worked hard with the babies in the days since they'd been retrieved from the gestational facility. To have lost one...

"Let me rephrase that. There's twenty-four, but Clarissa has taken to one in particular. She'd like us to be considered for CM-3." His hand shook a little, and David understood that his brother was seeking his assistance.

"Why should I?" It wasn't a demand or even a challenge, he was genuinely curious.

"Because we have a better knowledge of cybernetics. Because of what Colvert did to her. Because we will love the child, no matter what improvements they've made to the child."

David cocked his head to the side. "Why CM-3?"

"Because it reminds her of her siblings. Has the same eye color and hair. She thinks maybe the child is somehow genetically related to her. I'd like to run some scans, but knowing what I do..."

David's stomach churned, and he scrubbed his hand across his forehead. "Run the tests. If you can prove that, I'll make a case that you be given custody of CM without the other paperwork. So long as we can prove a link..."

"Thank you." Michael rose, the scrape of his chair on the floor loud and unsteady. "I'm not planning on telling Clarissa about this discussion until such time as..."

"That's probably a good idea. I'll talk to Daniella, let her know. How quickly can you run the tests?"

"If I start them immediately, we should have an answer tomorrow. Day after at the longest."

David nodded to Michael. "Okay then. I'll work on twenty-three at this stage and make backup plans only for CM."

"Thanks." Michael left, leaving David staring at the empty space where his brother had sat. So many changes. So many layers of machination and evil.

No answer to his own personal issues. He slammed the drink back and rose. This wasn't the way to find any answers.

E rin presented herself to Michael the next morning and waited for him to complete the examination. "So?"

"It's healing slowly because you keep overdoing it, Erin. If you'd rest, it would have time to complete the healing of blood vessels. Because you refuse to rest on your own, I'm going to be demanding desk duties only for you. I happen to know of a task that will require an extra set of hands."

Erin froze in shock. "Desk duties? There's a bloody war going on. I don't have time for—"

Michael shook his head, eyes glinting. "You will, because if you don't, an infection will set in and it'll take longer to heal. Each time you compromise the wound, you create a tiny tear just here." He pointed with a latex-covered finger to a small point where blood had oozed earlier. "This spot is the only one that hasn't fully completed closing, because you won't allow your body the time to rest."

Erin opened her mouth to argue, but he raised a hand.

"No. I'm not joking, McNally. Now, present yourself to the nursery, and I'll contact your superior."

Shock rippled. The nursery. Dammit, that's where David would be today. She closed her eyes briefly. "Surely there's something else..."

The pleading in her voice captured Michael's attention; she knew because his eyes widened. "Take it or leave it. And before you ask, I'll put you on enforced sick leave if you don't comply with this order. They're your choices."

She bared her teeth, inhaled deeply, and stood up straighter. "Fine. Desk duties."

He grinned at the tight way she spoke. "That's a good choice. Run along, and I'll see you again in a week."

She stalked from the room and headed to the nursery, surprised to see a line up at the doorway, David guarding the way. "Ladies and gentleman, you'll be assigned numbers and meeting times. We want to get through this as quickly as we can, so we'll can arrange secondary meetings with those we consider suitable once we've perused your applications. Please take a number from Clarissa. She'll allocate an interview time that's suitable for all of us for an initial meeting and to receive the detailed applications."

Some muttered while others simply shrugged and moved in Clarissa's direction, then Erin moved forward.

"Hey! Wait your turn," called a woman, and she turned to face them.

"I'm here to assist Agent Villede, not looking to adopt."

"Sure," muttered another, but Erin ignored them and marched up to David.

"Desk duties. I'm here to assist you." She refused to meet his eyes though, waiting for him to make some kind of remark about her being where she belonged, with him. *Yada yada yada.*

"Okay then, start with creating files for all those who wish to apply with Clarissa. Grab the forms and hand them out. Let them know we need them returned at the time of the interview fully completed."

She moved and he followed her, grabbing a seat and waiting as she lowered herself into it.

"Our first round is this afternoon. You can be crowd and diary control then, so no one interrupts. Clarissa would probably also welcome your assistance with the bathing and feeding routines."

She frowned at his dismissal. *Can it really be this easy? Would he allow them to be just workmates?*

David thrust a pen and box of folders at her then moved away to answer questions from waiting applicants, and Clarissa quirked an eyebrow at her before they become far too busy for her to dwell on personal problems.

D avid glanced at the briefing pages Daniella placed in front of the gathered team, more than a little aware that McNally had chosen to move to the furthest end of the table, as far away as from him as she could possibly get. He scanned the document as Daniella spoke.

"Our sources tell us that the loss of the infants has hurt them and their long-term planning. They're scrambling to replace the maturational chambers, though we have it on good authority that it will take some time. Their research files, decoded by Maylin, have yielded a lot of useful information. The professor will read them over and put together a briefing paper in a language we can understand and use. Dr. Windhower will work with him, and we hope to have some idea of the long-term ramifications for the children soon. We are also tugging on lines that give us an idea who is financially backing this project. If we can stop the cash flow, we might be able to mortally wound them."

"We still don't know who is behind—" David commented and smiled when Daniella turned to him, her smile tight.

"We now have an idea. Digging through the records of our main players so far, including Colvert, Ellis Corvino, and Joseph Olante." She stopped when David frowned. "Ah, you weren't here on the base for that portion of our investigations. Okay, let me briefly rehash it for you. Colvert's accident put him into the same sphere as Ellis Corvino, the headmaster of Eastcliffe. His association also stretched to Major Joseph Olante, who, as it tuns out, was selling intelligence back to us. We can extrapolate then that somehow they intersect with the person who has the ready cash reserves to back this project. Jonah, can you explain that?"

Jonah stood, moved to the door, and turned off the lights as the flare of the projector loomed on the wall. "What we know is they both grew up in the Eastcliffe Asylum. They then attended the public school until they went their separate ways, yet they never lost touch, seeing themselves as brothers, of a kind. When Corvino was injured he came into contact with Colvert. For a short while all three were in the same circles, and I believe that's when they came into contact with the backer. Colvert has a number of connections to high-ranking political, military, and financial minds. But taking a scatter gun approach and running through the PolSearch system, I've been able to narrow this down to about a dozen possible suspects. But it's not like we can simply head over and interrogate them. By demanding their cooperation, we run the risk of tipping them off."

Jonah paused, letting the information sink in, and David chanced a glance at Erin. She was furiously making notes on her pad, a frown stretching across her forehead, and for a moment, he wanted to reach over and brush it away. The urge passed as Jonah cleared his throat.

"We need to be sure of our ground before we reach that point, then shut down any way they can alert our ongoing quarry, because once we find the financial backer, I'm fairly sure we'll find the head of this plot. David, I know you're dealing with the infants' placements, but I need you and McNally to dig into the history of these people too. If Sevres and Fairburn have time, they can also assist. We need to run both programs in tandem, because once the infants are placed, we'll be able to move full speed ahead on whatever you find. The truth is, we have too many crucial personnel tied up with placing these children."

Jonah scratched his head, and David understood he was dealing with the million thoughts and threads that would be warring for space in his mind.

"I'm sending details to your personal communications systems based on these updated tasks," Jonah continued. "I want to keep all our information private, so absolutely nothing goes into the official communications systems until I say otherwise. Maylin is ensuring the privacy of our communications. Drop your devices to her and she'll install an encrypted comms system in there. Keep the comms program purely for these tasks."

David grimaced and handed his personal unit to Maylin. With a few quick moves, she downloaded a program then handed it back with a grunt. She then moved on to deal with the next as David opened the program, found the incoming file, and accessed it.

With a nod, David spoke to the team assembled. "I've got interviews tomorrow from nine until about two. We'll gather in the computer lab in the hospital after that to continue the process of digging into backgrounds. Michael, I'll need that lab locked-down for the foreseeable future. My team, Clarissa, Daniella, Jonah, and yourself the only exceptions. Maylin, can you unlink them from the systems, and retrofit them, so we can access what we need without tipping off anyone attempting to hack them?"

The Asian woman scoffed. "You haven't even thought of the ways I can increase the security. I'll be there."

Michael nodded at David who turned to Sevres and Fairburn. "You're not currently assigned to anything, are you?"

Fairburn cleared his throat. "We're supposed to be meeting with the commandant of the naval facility to talk about reinforcing their defenses."

David made some quick calculations and scrawled a notation on the paper pad beside him. "Franklin, can you cover that for Sevres and Fairburn, since your partner is now unavailable?"

His friend nodded. "Yeah, I can do that."

"Good, I'll send the updates out to whoever requires them, Jonah." David shifted in his seat.

Erin raised her hand, and David watched, interested in what she had to add. "During my surveillance with Franklin at Eastcliffe, it occurred to me that they are already hacking our systems. I think that includes our vid-feeds. On that basis, if we are carrying out any further surveillance, I would suggest we rely on non-electronic systems. I found an old spyglass in the commandant's office. It's low-tech and easy to use. As we drove by, we could see the numbers of children massing. They're not on alert yet, but we need to find out more. While we were surveilling, I was able to pinpoint the entry and exit I believe they're using."

David nodded. "Actually, I'd agree. The longer we can keep them guessing what we're up to…"

Jonah made a note on his whiteboard. "Excellent thinking, McNally. Let me see what I can do about getting some more of those…what did you call them again?"

"Spyglasses. You might get more from the naval facility. They were traditionally used on ships, I believe," Erin added.

Pleasure and pride speared David. Erin was far more capable and strategic thinking than many of those in more advanced positions.

"Good. Let's call this time then, and we'll reconvene at a later date. Send me updates as you have them through Maylin's comm program." Daniella stood and those assembled followed suit.

They left, most immediately, but David waited behind until he, Jonah, and Daniella remained. He cleared his throat. "Jonah? I need to talk to Daniella for a moment. Something non-operational."

Jonah cocked his head to the side. "Daniella?"

"It's fine. Grab me a coffee, and I'll be upstairs in a few minutes." David and Daniella waited until the door closed.

"So, what's up?" she asked.

"I spoke to Michael last night. He's running some tests, but it could be one of these children is based on Clarissa's genetic code."

His sister jerked at his bald words. "*Oh.* Oh shit!" Her eyes widened.

"They want to adopt the child if that's the case. I've asked him to go ahead and run the DNA testing that will prove or disprove the theory. There are more applicants than infants, but to be honest, of all those who are applying, theirs is probably the one I'd be most likely to place without question. Not because he's our brother, but because no one else will understand about the nano-tech and the emotional toll involved. I think they'll be more able to cope with the fallout that will likely come later on. But you need to sign off on that, under the circumstances." He waited, watching as his sister absorbed the information.

"And if the child isn't?"

David was ready for the query. "I still think they're the best placed to cope. No existing children, meaning the child will have time to form a strong attachment. They both have experience of the non-biological systems and the mental repercussions." He'd thought long and hard about how to prove his case.

She took a moment, moving around the room, thinking. He understood she was weighing up the pros and cons of what he'd presented. On a sigh, Daniella nodded. "I'll want something in writing outlining the steps taken, and I want a copy of the results the minute you have them."

He released a breath he hadn't realized he'd held onto. "You've got it. Thanks."

Her glance was surprised. "What for?"

"Understanding the situation. For realizing it's not about favoritism or nepotism or..." He felt foolish when she smiled.

"That's because I'm who and what I am, David. Years of practice and understanding your thought processes help too." She moved over and gave him a quick hug then exited the room. At the door she stopped and glanced back at him. She opened her mouth then shut it, shook her head, and left him alone in the room.

Erin peered at the screen and rubbed her eyes. "I've got Mika Davyon. Anyone have any background?" she called to the team gathered in the small room.

"No, but Marylou Gantry is possible, given her position as head of the World Bank. She's got access to networks and the know-how to head something like this up." Fairburn tugged at his dirty blond hair and growled.

"Keep doing that, man, and it'll all fall out someday." Sevres spoke with a creole accent that still surprised Erin even after working with him for over four years.

"So, let's put Gantry on our list. I don't have any real feeling about

Davyon. I'm going to look into Xar-Yin because there's something about her that feels off." Erin reclined back in the seat and brought up the picture of the Asian woman. In her fifth or sixth decade—and that was hard to pin down these days—she oozed some kind of superiority that left Erin itching. She snorted. *That may be my personal issues drawing conclusions.*

"If you take Xar-Yin, then I've got Boris Grevanov. Multi-trillion-aire with interests in military and health services. He might fit the bill too." Sevres rose and added the name to the list with a quick *"sousoute."*

Erin ignored the comment; she was used now to his odd comments and swearing in the creole language of his father. "Right, let's dive into their backgrounds, keeping an eye out for any other intersecting characters, donations, or odd interests and the like."

Erin opened up the PolSearch. She was aware Maylin had managed to hide the browsing histories for these units, allowing them to search with immunity, hidden from the systems that would track ordinary usage. The information they sought was far too dangerous for anyone, including other authorities, to know about. If anyone tipped the wrong people off, it might end their mission in a heartbeat.

Her fingers tapped the keyboard as she gathered information on family connections, sources of financial data, and ran connecting checks on social media platforms. Nothing jumped out at her, but she knew this was barely scratching the surface. Every person tagged would receive deeper investigation. This merely allowed them to weed out those who didn't meet their normal criteria at this point. Their names wouldn't be completely removed from the list, only shoved to a lower-level list.

She was exhausted and rubbing aching eyes. By eight, exhaustion dragged at her. "Anything?"

"One or two links that are worth following up. I just don't know though. I can't see that the answer is going to jump out at us and wave a flag going *pick me*." Fairburn spoke drily, and she snorted.

"I'm not convinced my target is the right one. I have a few others that interest me. I'll prioritize them and start again in the morning after the interviews."

Sevres nodded. "I'm off to the bar for a drink, so who'll join me?" Erin shook her head and watched as Fairburn accepted the invitation.

They'll both have sore heads in the morning, she mused then turned off her screen. She stood and stretched, her side twinging but not with the same depth she'd been experiencing in the last few days. Perhaps Michael had been right. She needed time to heal. It just sat badly, not being on the street in the thick of things as she liked.

Leaving the lab, she engaged the lock, palming the key Michael had popped on the side, and was nearly through the front door when a hail from David stopped her in his tracks. He stood in the hall, his face devoid of emotion, like someone with a secret they didn't want to share. It piqued her interest. Whether or not he had something she wanted to know though, was another question.

"Got a minute?"

God, she wished she could refuse him. But she'd been leaving the hospital, and Fairburn and Sevres weren't with her. It didn't take a lot to work out that she was heading for her tiny room on the base, and because she rarely mixed he'd known she wasn't heading somewhere.

That and the *desk duties* tag meant she wasn't going to training or anything else urgent. Erin turned with ill grace and looked at him, watching as he beckoned her. "Why?"

"Since you're involved with the infants, I thought you'd like to be on hand. The senator and Jonah will be here in a moment too." David's cryptic words intrigued her, so she followed him to the nursery.

Within minutes Daniella and Jonah had joined them, and David tugged a printout from his pocket and handed it to Daniella.

The wad of papers David handed over caught Erin's attention, and she waited, expecting an announcement of gravity.

"They're a match, Daniella." David's face wasn't wreathed in smiles, but the air around him suggested he'd made some great breakthrough. "Michael and Clarissa's suspicions were on track."

Daniella's smile was small.

I wonder what this is about.

Daniella cleared her throat. "Then our agreement stands. When do you want to—" She waved her hands toward the cots in rows, her gaze on David.

"I've already requested they join us," David answered.

Erin watched, confused for a brief moment. "What..."

"In a moment." David smiled, and that made focusing on the situation difficult because her heart lurched at the sudden twinkle in his eyes.

A knock on the door—soft enough to not wake the sleeping children—broke her realization that ignoring David would be an ongoing task. Something she'd have to work at forever. David opened the sliding door, and Clarissa and Michael entered the room, blinking with surprise to see those gathered.

"What's wrong? Is one of the babies ill?" Clarissa's hands balled, her face a mask, but the wobble of her lips betrayed her emotional turmoil.

"No. But we have some results we thought you'd like to know about. Michael?"

David's brother nodded and pulled Clarissa closer. She frowned. "What?"

David grinned. "Michael shared his suspicions that CM shared some genetic heritage with you, Clarissa. He arranged for tests to happen. He was right. CM does share genetic markers with you. To that end, and after speaking at length with Daniella, it's been decided that CM will be placed with you for adoption. Congrats, Mom and Dad."

The truth shocked Erin.

She'd never have expected that Clarissa would somehow be related any of these children. Her hand flew to her mouth. Her mind spun, putting together everything she knew.

Clarissa had been abducted. The person who'd done that had also owned an IVF laboratory. More than one. She'd been used as a guinea pig, and Erin knew that they'd implanted Clarissa more than once. Her gut churned. *What if the genetic tissue had been Clarissa's?*

Erin's gaze flew to David. He shook his head imperceptibly. Clearly that thought hadn't eluded him either.

"My child." Clarissa strode calmly to a particular cot, reached down and picked up the child. Her smile beatific. "Our child, Michael. What shall we call her?"

"Camille." His voice roughened, tears washing in his eyes, and yet Michael, in that moment, had never seemed quite so impressively male. Erin's heart melted for the couple.

Daniella cleared her throat. "Fine, we can attend to the paperwork in the morning. You'll need supplies—"

"I'd already ordered them." Michael cleared his throat as Daniella's eyes widened and rounded with shock.

"Oh. Okay then." And for the first time Erin saw a different and more uncertain Daniella.

With a nod, the couple turned, their new daughter carefully cradled in Clarissa's arms, and strode as a family from the room.

"Well, I think that concludes the evening." Jonah slid his hand around Daniella's waist and steered her from the room. Erin watched them leave, more than aware she was here in a silent room with David. And the twenty-three remaining infants who slept on, unaware of the gravity of the tableau that had just been played out.

"We should..." She waved toward the door, and he nodded.

"There'll be a night nurse in here soon to care for the others. Join me for a drink?" Erin bit her lip, proud to have been included in the tightly knit circle of his family but wary that he'd try to push for more. After all, she was no better than the children lying in the cots around her.

"No pressure. Just a drink. Please. You can even ask what I know you need an answer to."

Unable to speak, Erin nodded her agreement, and together they made their way out of the infirmary. Crossing the base, they headed for the Officer's Club.

CHAPTER THREE

*E*rin read the information on the screen, pleased the week had passed reasonably uneventfully. There had been several attacks by the children, in the town and some of the outlying farmlands, but nothing that hadn't been overcome by the troops assembled in local areas.

"A surprisingly easy week," said Maylin, their computer programmer. She was perched in the hallway beside Erin as she waited for her medical clearance from Michael. Maylin had assured her she was simply there to run a test on the clinic computers, and McNally found the woman interesting and engaging.

"Yes. Kind of odd really." Erin sighed and looked up the hall, wondering where Michael was.

"Odd? McNally, it seems you can't take a positive easily."

Erin glanced at the small woman. "It's a matter of experience. Usually things that appear easy on the surface have the biggest bite when it comes to things going wrong."

"I never would have tagged you for a fatalist, McNally. Oh well, I'll take the positive when I get it." Maylin grinned at her, and Erin simply shrugged.

The door to the clinic opened, and Michael beckoned Erin

within, so she rose, smoothed down her dress pants, and entered the small room. Michael took up a position before her, and at his gesture, she unfastened the blouse for his inspection of the wound site.

"Much better. The wound has had time to settle. Finally." He poked and prodded, made notations on the notepad on his desk. "I'm happy to return you to active service, surmising you don't undertake anything too strenuous, such as hand-to-hand or assisting in the lifting of something heavy. I want to see you again in a week for a further assessment."

Erin opened her mouth to remonstrate, but Michael held up his hand. "That's the only way I'm happy to mark you as ready for active duty, Agent McNally. Take it or leave it."

She grunted. "Okay. I'll take what I can get."

He plopped himself down on his seat, made a few swift notes on the file, and printed a form out. "Here's your clearance. You'll see I've listed your restrictions. See Marjorie at the desk on your way out, and she'll schedule your appointment and we'll send the report through to your direct superior."

Erin simply bared her teeth at that, knowing full well David would question any information he received. He'd questioned a lot of her choices the night they'd had drinks in the Officer's Club.

She shoved the folded paper into her back pocket, saluted, and swiftly left the room, feeling lighter than she had in some time. Her clearance meant she'd be able to participate once more in the field, instead of peering into a screen, looking for the financial backer.

It didn't matter that she and the crew had already managed to narrow down the field, her sense of achievement and fulfillment was tied to her work in the field. It was where she did her best work. She reveled in that.

The communicator in her pocket blared, and she tugged it out, looked at it, and groaned. *David*. Great. Just what she needed. It took a lot to not roll her eyes. Had he been checking her schedule again?

"McNally."

"Meet me at Jonah's office. He has something for us to check out."

The terse words stripped any personal concerns away. This was business. That came before anything else. Always had, and always would.

"On my way." Erin moved swiftly through the building and out into the grounds of the base, the cadence of the boots thudding on the asphalt music to her ears.

Crack. She stopped for a second, attempting to place the sound.

Crack. This time it was louder. Closer maybe. The thud of her heart speeding. *Crack!*

The sound echoed, and Erin gasped. Whatever it was, it didn't bode well. She started forward again, all the while her mind questioning, what was the noise and where was it coming from?

Patwang! The sound of a ricochet she knew well. She threw herself to the ground. "What the…"

She rolled, her eyes scanning the buildings, and in the shadow of one building she spied a child. One she hadn't seen before, lurking near Jonah's office window, the nose of a small caliber handgun incongruous.

McNally pushed up, hand spread as she gained her feet, then pushed off. Her legs pumped as she raced in the direction of the building.

Her mind moved into action mode, all the while her gaze locked on the outline of the child, moving as quickly and silently as she could.

Her movement caught the child's attention; it spun then moved deeper into the shadows. Erin pressed the button on the communicator in her hand, hoping like hell the redial function would kick in.

"Villede."

"Infiltrator, near Jonah's office. In pursuit. Backup required." She panted as she sprinted forward. At the point where she'd seen the child, she found no one there.

Footprints, small ones, were present, and she bent down, checking before once more looking up, seeking the child.

David's swearing echoed through the earpiece, but she glanced left and right, peering deep into the shadows.

A movement caught her attention, and she ducked as a projectile moved in her direction. Flattened on the ground, she looked up and noted the child jackrabbiting away in the direction of the boundary fencing.

If they got out...

She didn't let the rest of the thought form, intent on capturing the interloper, but the child was faster than she was, given she'd been out of action for some weeks and her fitness had suffered as a result.

At the fence, the child jumped, gripped the meshing, and hauled itself up and over, then was gone.

Erin stilled and swore. "Damn!"

Her hands hung loosely by her side as several others joined her, David among them.

"Where?"

"Got away." She panted out the words, hands moving to her hips as she bent forward, sucking in a lungful of oxygen. "They knew the layout of the base. They were bloody quick and didn't hang around for me to interrogate them."

She waited, concentrating on settling her racing heart.

The others milled around until David dismissed the military police with a flick of his hand and a curt word.

Erin straightened, then waited, eyes shadowed as she scanned the horizon. The vehicular traffic passing the base had slowed since the war's beginning, but not enough that crossing the road wouldn't have been without its dangers. The child hadn't waited, but moved as if they were sure of their direction, and along with the knowledge of just how dangerous these kids were, that also concerned her.

"What do you think they wanted?" David's query caught her attention.

"They had what appeared to be a gun and were hanging by Jonah's office. I didn't see them firing, and I'd bet they didn't discharge the weapon, but I think we should check for bugs. They seem to like the electronic tracking, using it widely."

He stared at her. "You think they broke in, carried a loaded weapon, but simply bugged the window?"

She blushed at his words. Even to her ears it sounded like

nonsense. "We won't know until we check, will we?" She made to stomp off, but David stopped her.

"I know you're upset, but logically it doesn't make sense."

She sighed. "I know, it's just a feeling I have. I don't suppose you happen to have a scanner on hand, do you?"

He stared then shook his head. "As it happens, I do. That is why they call me ever- ready."

For a moment, a bubble of mirth rose. "I don't know anyone who calls you that."

He touched the side of his nose. "I know plenty who do. I'll grab it from the glove compartment of my vehicle. Better yet, I'll give you a lift and we can discuss what else I plan to investigate once we're headed for the office."

He led her to the compact unit, and she clambered inside, settling against the cushioning, resting her aching body. "So?'

"It seems Colvert has an active account with the World Bank. We have leads on his others, but he's using an involved tree of trusts and businesses to hide his investments. I want you to go with me—incognito as one of my accountants. I want to see if we can't access the hard data. I have a warrant created by the First Justice."

Erin glanced at him. "A warrant from the First Justice?" *Rare as hen's teeth.*

"Okay, it's an excellent forgery." His deadpan delivery had her shaking her head.

"Your incorrigible."

"I know. That's why you like me, McNally."

She laughed. What else was there to do? "In uniform?"

He sobered at her query. "Soft clothes. We don't want to be made as agents or military. They won't cooperate if there are any questions as to the validity and our time will be short."

Hmm. "Let's check for this bug first."

He shook his head. "This one takes priority. I'll send a team to Jonah's office and have it evacuated until it's been cleared."

Erin scowled, knowing she'd rather be in the thick of things, but what he said made sense too. They wouldn't expect something like this on the back of a base incursion.

"Fine. Drop me at the accommodation unit. I have suitable clothing there." She had, having packed a selection of work and personal clothes, unsure exactly what to expect or what she might return to at a later date.

"Good." He turned in that direction and stopped the vehicle. "Twenty minutes back here?"

"Yeah, I can manage that." She climbed out. "Weapons?"

"Secreted but yes. It's hard to know if we'll need them."

Fifteen minutes passed, and Erin was waiting by the car as David descended the steps. She lounged there, clad in a pair of black slacks, blue blouse, and flat, black shoes he was sure she'd chosen with a view to how quickly she could run. Her tightly belted coat concealed a small pistol in a holster under her arm.

He'd seen her move in pursuit of the child, legs and arms moving in smooth concert.

She'd moved like a cougar. Long, powerful movements and an innate grace.

"You're quick," he said.

Her smile was tight. "You said twenty minutes. Why muck around?"

Those words confirmed his thoughts about her level of organization. He'd taken only the time necessary to change, rooting in the cupboard for something suitable. Tidy rooms had never been his thing, and that hadn't changed into adulthood for all his work-life was ruthlessly laid out.

"We'll take Michael's car. It's reasonably nondescript and won't arouse suspicion." He gestured toward the parking lot at the end of the carpark, and she trailed behind him.

David fished into his pocket and retrieved the key. The car beeped as he approached, but before he could reach for the door, Erin stopped him. "We should check for bugs. Can't be too careful now."

The tiny scanner she hadn't held previously beeped and glowed blue. "So, we're clear?"

She nodded. "Did anyone check the building?"

"I contacted the military police and requested a full inspection. You were right. A tiny listening bug had been attached to the windowsill, underneath the window. You've got a sneaky mind." It wasn't quite what he meant to say, but she grinned as if he'd complimented her.

"You should know by now that it's what I do best, along with running and hand-to- hand."

David groaned as he started the car. "No hand-to-hand for you according to Michael." He revved the vehicle. "Let's get moving before we run into someone who's wise to our moves."

Her laugh tinkled, and he frowned.

"Why are you laughing?" he asked.

"I'm just pleased to be back in the field." With those words, she sobered. "Do you think we'll find anything useful?"

He shrugged. "I don't know. It's a long shot, but with the morass of links and ties, we need a break to help us track the funds. Without that, we're poking at dead-ends. We need to find the financial backers and take them out before they can launch a full-out offensive. Until we lock them down, they'll just keep pouring money into the problem, and we've got limited finances. Only what Daniella managed to sequester before they stripped access to official accounts."

Erin frowned and looked out the window, and David wondered what was going on inside her mind.

The woman was a dichotomy.

Ruthless and fast, critical thinking among her skills along with an empathy that still surprised him. Her hand-to-hand was exceptional as were her weapons skills.

"Why did you join the agency?"

She turned, hair whipping around her face, to look at him. "I wanted to make a difference. I'd been a pawn and plaything, and giving something back made sense to me."

He considered her answer. "You do that every day."

Erin blinked at him. "Uh, thanks, I think."

They continued the drive in silence, taking in the signs of the abandoned stores and where throngs of people had once milled. Instead of throngs of people, now there were possibly a dozen or so moving rapidly, regularly checking around them.

They continued for a while, drawing closer to the city. On the outskirts he pulled up to a nondescript building and shoved an ID into her hands. "Here you go, Ms Erin Bellamy. Your identification. We work for Matthison, Stone, and Valley."

She cocked an eyebrow. "That's reaching high."

"Family friends. The ID will stand at least an initial check."

She stepped from the vehicle, waited as he retrieved a black attaché case from the rear of the vehicle, then moved with him toward the doors.

E rin wasn't too sure about the cover, but David seemed comfortable with it, so she inwardly shrugged.

Once they moved inside, they stilled at a large marble desk, and David affected a befuddled air as he rattled around in the bag.

"Ms Bellamy and Mr. Messingham here to retrieve documentation for Colvert, Jeremy."

The woman on the desk looked down her nose at David from the high chair she sat perched in behind the desk. "You'll need authorization or warrant."

"I have that." He slid the paper onto the gleaming counter and waited as she scanned it.

"Let me get a director down here." She turned smoothly, and Erin's belly knotted.

Had they somehow betrayed themselves already?

The woman talked into a tiny headset, and Erin had to stop herself from hopping from one foot to the other.

When she turned, the woman had a tight smile on her lips. "Director Samring will be with you in a moment. Please take a seat."

With one swift motion, the woman gestured to the seating to her left, and they obeyed, sinking into the plush blue chairs for designated VIP guests, Erin thought.

Time passed slowly, as if the world ceased rotating, until a tiny man approached them, lean and with thinning, gray hair. "You're here from which firm, please?"

"Matthison, Stone, and Valley. In Torvingston." They both rose.

The man's brows rose. "Ah. Your authorization?"

"The young lady on the counter has it."

Samring waited as the woman extended the sheet of paper. He scanned it, then nodded. "This appears to be in order. What exactly do you require?"

"The last twelve months' worth of transactions for the accounts of Jeremy Colvert."

"For what purposes?" Samring's eyes flared, and Erin contained a shudder, wondering if he'd worked out their mission was bogus.

"He's being detained by the alliance. We need to prepare a case for his release, including proving there was no way he could possibly be bound to anything inappropriate or illegal."

"Wait one moment." Samring beckoned one of the men hovering behind the counters, waiting for patrons.

"Daxter here will assist you. Should you have any further queries, please do not hesitate to contact us." With a tight bow, Samring melted away, leaving them both stunned.

A tall man, blue-eyed with short blond hair approached. "I was requested to print out the transactions for Mr. Jeremy Colvert. Would you need his checking or savings accounts?"

Erin grappled quickly with the fact they hadn't found them all. "All of them, thanks. There could be transactions in both, according to the information we've received. It's wise to be prepared." She grinned, she hoped, in a friendly fashion, and watched as he reciprocated, puffing out his chest a little more. A quick glance at his hands showed no marks of ceremonial pairing, or rings for those far more traditional like Clarissa and Michael or Daniella and Jonah.

Erin didn't look at David but felt the negativity pulsing off him in waves. Accepted it, then ignored it. They were there to complete the mission, and that's exactly what she'd do.

Daxter ushered them forward, then pulled out a seat for her, and she floated into it, playing her part to the hilt.

"It must be a good place to work. Lots of people to interact with."

Settling himself into the seat opposite her, his fingers finding spots on the keyboard, Daxter started tapping. "I haven't been here too long, but yeah. They're all nice, if a little stuffy." He grinned at her, and she poured a little more into the character she'd assumed, grinning back at him.

"Oh, so you haven't had any interaction with Mr. Colvert?" Erin pushed deeper, hoping to find out something, thinking it odd that they'd ask a new staff member to access the information. Something smelled strange, and she shifted in her chair, turned to David. "I left my communicator in the car. Would you mind retrieving it?"

He'd know exactly what that meant, that they'd possibly been compromised. If one of them was able to get out, then it was better than losing two operatives, she told herself, shying away from the truth that it was better that she be caught than him.

David's eye glinted, but her query left him no choice but to either blow both their covers or acquiesce. He rose. "I'll be back in a moment."

The minute he was gone, Erin turned back to Daxter, who had a questioning look on his face. "Is he your boss or..."

The words hung in the air, and she controlled the groan of dissatisfaction at his reading of the situation. "We don't have that kind of relationship," she assured him, trying to keep to the truth as much as possible.

"Oh." He brightened considerably, and the chatter of the printer began, shooting page after page of information at them. It was only a minute or two when he collected the sheaf and passed it over to her, then slid a card into her hands. "I'm free Saturday night. Would you join me for drinks?"

She'd played her part too well, knew she'd have to shut him down carefully. "I'm, uhhh, involved in a big case at the moment. Socializing is something I don't have a lot of time for at this point. But look, how about when it's done, I can get in contact with you?" The seeds of a thought were gathering in her brain. Holding onto the pages, she rose and smiled. "Thanks for this. We'll be in touch."

She shoved the papers into the black case and moved swiftly, hoping like hell she'd get out before the police or children descended.

At the door she breathed deeply and plunged into the fresh air. David waited in the car, and she all but flew in his direction and dove into the vehicle, shoving the case to her feet. "Just drive. We can talk on the way."

David had the car screaming out into the street, the set of his lips cold and hard, wicked planes of white flesh. He didn't say a word, didn't need to. Anger rolled off him. She knew exactly what he was thinking.

"Look, Daxter could be useful. He invited me to drinks and gave me his direct number. I'm sure we could groom him as a contact." Erin realized it sounded downright foolish this trying to explain to the man beside her. Her chattering was about building a rapport so Daxter wouldn't question what they requested, and meanwhile, David was steaming that she'd sent him out.

"Fine." David's answering nod incensed her.

Erin fought to keep her cool. The old adjunct of not getting involved with a workmate bit her fair and square on the arse now, because she'd rather not go to drinks with Daxter when she was wholly wound up in… She halted the thought before it could grow.

The knowledge that she'd fought it damn hard but still, somehow, crawled knee-deep into the middle of a tangled, personal relationship with her boss slashed at her. *I didn't ask for this!*

Life hadn't done her any favors. From the time she'd been born, abandoned at the hospital, to now, not one aspect of her life had been normal.

The authorities had attempted to foster her several times, but it never worked out. She was either too quiet or too athletic, not studious enough for the families' liking, or too distracting for the males of the family. In the end, she'd embraced the orphanage she'd ended up in, thankful for the relative stability and impersonality that came with it.

She'd finished school, applied to the military. They'd rejected her with a 'too cerebral' tag but had shunted her into the agency program instead.

That was where she'd found the sense of belonging she'd all but given up on. She'd made herself one of the boys and risen through the ranks.

Then she'd met David.

Far too high for her, she'd told herself and directed herself to instead focus on her career.

"When do you plan to meet with him?" David's question woke her from the introspection, and she jumped a little.

"What? Oh, I don't. Not now anyway. I'm thinking we can dangle him on the hook, see if we can't get him to share information with us. He's open to a meeting, so perhaps down the track he'll be useful to us."

"Is that all you see men for? Usefulness?" He spat the words at her.

This time she did roll her eyes and clench her fists. "Oh, for... He could be a good contact at the bank if we need them. We have a mission to focus on. You, as my boss, should be more concerned about that than anything else."

Erin turned back to the window, ending the conversation and watching as they swung back into the base.

When the vehicle drew to a gentle stop, Erin jumped out, grabbing the case and heading to the office area in the clinic where the rest of the team was already hard at work.

David followed her, but she continued to ignore him. If she spoke to him right now, she'd likely say something inappropriate, so she kept silent.

At the office, she slammed inside, slid the case onto the desk in the center of the room, then plonked herself down on the chair. With a few rapid keystrokes, Erin woke the computer and logged into the system.

Several communications awaited, the beeping of a red icon in the top left-hand corner glowing. Hovering over it informed her two emails waited.

She clicked and blinked as the screen exploded in color. A laughing caricature of a face echoed loudly, and she reared back. "Fuck! I've been hacked!"

Fairburn spun in the seat beside her. "How did that happen?"

She sprang out of her chair. "I have no idea!" Now she seethed and sank her fingertips into her hair. "This is absolutely beyond the limit!"

David hovered, his gaze narrowed at the image on the screen. "We need Maylin to see if she can track it." When Erin made to turn off the computer, he barked, "Leave it."

Fuming, Erin pulled her chair back and held onto the padding. "Fine. But once we find out who did this, I'll burn them." Her fit of temper began melting away, and she tottered to the coffee stand in the corner and poured one for herself as she waited.

The small Asian woman scurried in. "Who got hacked? I put every kind of limiter on those machines, except the XL-4 scanner program."

Erin pointed to her machine, and Maylin dropped herself into the seat, where she tapped a couple of keys and grinned.

"They're good, but I'm better," Maylin stated. "I need a communicator and notepad." Sevres jumped to comply, and for the first time Erin realized he rarely spoke but was always the first to fulfill requests. When Erin glanced closer she realized he also blushed the tiniest bit around this woman. A grin edged over Erin's face. *Another possible fool down for the count!*

Erin turned back, mesmerized as she watched as Maylin battled away. Her tapping in short bursts, screens flashing up, and command prompts filling the screen.

Ten minutes passed, and Erin sipped her coffee.

Twenty minutes later, Maylin pushed away from the computer. "I've got them!"

The screen that flicked up was one Erin knew well. A tiny pop-up flashed and an IP address, numbers separated by periods that Maylin explained would be able to be followed. She noted down the details, then closed the screen and opened a browser window and entered the numbers.

"Location Eastcliffe. Give me an hour or so on my own system, and I'll even have an address of the computer."

Erin shook her head, amazed that the woman had achieved so much in so little time.

"Was that a difficult to track hack? I mean, was it a high-level…"

The woman giggled. "Not really. Some of it's older tech, so I'd say whoever it is that initiated the hack is probably still learning." Her smile died away. "If it's one of the children, in a year or two, they'll be formidable. They need to be stopped."

David strode to the computer. "How did they crack this system and know it's one of our machines?"

Maylin sighed. "There's a specific syntax we all use when dealing with computers. I'd say they've been running a tagging program on the web, checking for the syntax of our search strings. It's not hard, a simple cookie-like program that self-unpacks within the systems it detects using those parameters."

"Can you do a breakdown, so we know what to avoid?"

"Sure. It'll maybe take me a couple of hours to work them out, but I'll send your details via the secure communication program I installed on your hand-helds. I suggest that everyone closes down for the night and allow my team to run diagnostics and check to see if anyone else has been attacked."

David nodded. "That makes sense. Everyone, early mark. We'll be back here tomorrow, oh-eight-hundred hours."

No one grumbled or raised concerns, and Fairburn and Sevres began turning off the systems.

"No! Don't power down, let me access your immediate caches and run my checks."

Fairburn grunted while Sevres nodded then took their cups to the sink for washing later.

After carrying them over, he left quickly, likely thinking if they waited there was a chance David might find them some alternative tasks.

Maylin excused herself so that only David and Erin remained in the office.

He cleared his throat. "Look, I have to apologize for my behavior earlier. I realize it made no sense, and in my defense, I'm not sure I could have contained it."

Erin shook her head. "We'll forget it, sir. Now, if I'm dismissed, I think I'll head over to the physical training center, do some laps, and see if I can't build up my stamina."

He stared at her then nodded, but not before she saw the regret on his face. "Of course." She left the room, unready to acknowledge just how much it hurt to do so.

****

David cursed himself as several kinds of fool. Getting involved on the job was one of those vital rules that you weren't supposed to ignore, and yet here he was, doing just that. There was no way to ignore the attraction between them. It slammed into him like a brick wall every time he looked at Erin, and it was getting in the way of her doing the job too.

Watching her follow the actions of the woman dealing with the hacking reminded him forcefully of the way she tackled any aspect of her job, with total concentration. Just like she'd done earlier with the young man in the bank. Finding a way to connect then use it to their best advantage.

He had to rein himself in, he told himself. He'd already scared her away, and soon, if this continued, she'd be unable to complete her role. That would endanger her.

The prospect shamed him.

CHAPTER FOUR

*E*rin settled back at the computer, a printout beside her showing her usual search string makeup and how to mask them. Maylin was a wizard with technology, and Erin was pleased that the woman was on their side.

"Let's see. If I try finances, philanthropic backing, and exclude Colvert at this point, what do I get?" The screen blinked, and a larger number of hits rolled down. Four hundred and twenty-one hits. She hissed through her teeth. "Add refined data, Jeremy Colvert, medical." And the list narrowed to forty-seven. "Now I'm getting somewhere."

She started excluding those they'd already investigated and grinned at the total of fourteen left. So Maylin's instructions worked a treat.

"Print list and delete current data from cache."

The computer flashed a warning and she over-rode it with a tap of the keyboard. By the time the team arrived in the office, she'd already placed the allocations for checking on everyone's desks. "There's a refined list for everyone. I think if we run a detailed study on each and every one, we'll get a clearer idea of who should remain on our shortlists. Check financial transactions in and out over the last six months, then we'll go deeper on those who look likely. I want to see hidden accounts, investments, and property that seems out of the ordinary or above their pay grade. Any snippet of information will help." She started to roll back to the computer.

"Check affiliations, including political and peak bodies, to the list of searches." David had entered the room on silent feet, and she startled, the seat jumping beneath her.

"Got it!" Fairburn turned to his screen, grunted as he checked the papers beside him, then began to tap away while David settled himself at the fourth unit and began running his own searches on their previous hits.

David would pick up the slack when they'd moved on, she knew. It was the way he worked, taking their efforts and refining them. It was a system that worked incredibly well for the team.

Erin cleared her mind from the maze of concerns about them and settled into the rhythm, checking files, requesting information, and sending notations to the file as things popped.

One name returned a scant three possible ties, but her gut told her they were weak, so she slid that biography to the side and reached for another.

Another searcher tagged fifteen, and she gritted her teeth, delving into their history, including a failed relationship with a doctor. That file she marked and flicked over to David with a list of why she felt this person was a possible target.

The work was tiring and monotonous. They broke at midday and headed for the mess, their work area secured until they returned. The afternoon was the same, files checked.

In her own mind, she was sure that while she'd possibly found some connections, none were enough to take the chance of a full PolSearch, as right now what they did barely scratched the surface. To go deeper would trigger alarms.

"Erin? Could you come here for a moment?" David's voice echoed, and the entire team turned their heads in his direction. Erin stood and made her way to him. "This one? The failed relationship, they have shared assets even though they haven't been together for very long."

She leaned close and read what he could see on screen. "Let's take a look at the board of directors. It's an Eastcliffe located company, and that keeps popping up as a location of interest."

David scratched his head. "True, but I wonder if that's by design, a red herring, or whether we've got lucky and stumbled on a thread."

His hands flew across the keyboard, and she watched, his fingers sure and firm but without stabbing at the keys.

He set the parameters, checked the clock that popped up in the window, and leaned back in his seat. "I think we should stop after this. Guys, it's after nineteen-hundred hours. Go eat, and we'll be back here tomorrow at oh-seven-hundred. I'm building a theory, and we should brainstorm it."

Fairburn and Sevres shut down the machines then left the room.

"Not joining them?" David asked Erin.

She shook her head. "I want to see what you've found first. I think you could be right to question the location. It seems too pat. Too easy. The truth is never easy."

He turned in her direction, blinked slowly. "Why?"

The words startled her. "Why what?"

"You said the truth is never easy. Why is that?"

Erin shrugged, suddenly uncomfortable with the words she'd spoken. Based on her experiences, truth was rarely easy to understand or accepted without question.

"Erin?" The mesmerizing green of his eyes beckoned, and suddenly unsure of herself, she stepped back at the same time as the machine beeped, telling her the results of his run had come through.

He swiveled in his seat, once more giving the machine his attention, and she felt overwhelming relief that he hadn't pushed her. "What did you find?" she asked.

David grunted. "Their interconnected. It's an extended family connection between her and Colvert."

"Eww!" The sound of disgust echoed, and he chuckled.

"Royal families used to do it all the time."

"No. Just, no." She shook her head. "How sure are you?"

"Colvert's sister, Annalise, was also a board member, along with four of the other cousins. I'd say this is a hangover from the family, but I'll run a deeper search on—"

"I didn't know Colvert had a sister." Erin frowned and rubbed the ache that began between her eyes.

"She died nine years ago. A motor vehicle accident."

"Hmm. That's mighty timely, right? It's right about when he started shunting money into his IVF clinics big time. Began the mission, if you will."

"You're thinking she knew something?" David stood, the chair scooting across the floor. "I've created a printout. We can take a look at all the information over dinner and discuss it."

David stalked to the printer as Erin watched, bemused that he expected her to just be there over a meal. Either he was backing off finally—and she wasn't sure how she felt about that—or he was taking another tack to spending time with her. That was far more unsettling.

Right now there was a mission to complete. They'd track these bloody finances if it killed them, then get the bastard who'd put them in this position. The only thing was, given the danger, it could really be the last thing she did if they weren't careful.

David cleared his throat, and she startled to realize he'd noticed her wool-gathering and had powered down the machines and waited for her. "Ready?"

Unable to say anything, Erin simply nodded her agreement and followed him from the room.

David wasn't sure if he should be pleased she'd agreed to dinner with him or be dismayed that she'd been so totally engrossed in her own thoughts before they'd left their temporary office that she'd agreed to the meal. It might be in the mess hall, but the opportunity to just be with her was a boon.

Erin was an insightful woman, and it seemed that some of the prickly barriers she'd put up with him were because of her childhood, not that he knew why they were in place. He also felt sure it wasn't yet time for her to open up and that would only come after he'd built her trust.

Frustration at himself shackled his emotions, and every now and again he'd have to back away from his connection to her. Then he'd likely have to refocus his defenses before trying something new.

David settled the thick sheaf of papers on the table between them. "These are my deeper scans on the names the three of you sent my way. I don't think there's much of depth in any, except Melony Davison, the one you gave me. Sevres sent me Georg Fiers, and Fairburn tagged Xi Lin Wong. Their financials aren't out of the ordinary for their positions. They each move in pseudo political circles and have connection with R and D companies. Any of them could fit the bill. I'm thinking though that Celeste Landry is certainly a contender with her former relationship."

Erin mumbled, "I still think that's just sick!"

David smiled at the disgust in her tone. "She moves in the right circles, knows all the people. But I'm not reading her as someone who'd been involved in overthrowing the government. Her family interests include several community health centers, disadvantaged youth shelters, and..."

Erin tapped her finger against her lips. "What if it's not her specifically? What if she's merely the conduit?"

David considered her idea. "Would be worth a look." He scrawled a notation on the file, then closed the heavy cover. "We should eat. The stew will be getting cold."

He gave his attention to the spoon, studiously avoiding looking at her, refusing to trigger a negative reaction. This was as close as he'd been since the mistaken move on her in his home.

"You know, I know what you're thinking, David."

He almost choked and looked up at her. "You do?"

"Sure. I mean it must be hard for you, after the way you'd lived your life to be able to understand the actions of Colvert. Look at what he did to your sister-in-law, Clarissa. To countless other unwilling victims. The children too, but we need to put aside what we know to

47

understand their thought processes." She had speared a piece of meat and held it over the bowl, frowning.

"That's not quite what I was thinking." He couldn't contain a small grin.

"Life isn't black and white, but lots of shades of gray. Getting darker right now, but that's okay, I'm used to that." She popped the meat into her mouth and chewed.

Erin cocked her head, and he considered her words carefully. "Dark. What do you mean?"

"Well, some of us, we've had a not very easy start to life. Sometimes it stays with us. Makes it easier to interpret the darker things in life. Means we can read it better than others. I think that's me. But hey, that's a conversation for another time. Tell me what you were thinking then." She gazed intently at him.

Her words reinforced his concerns that she wasn't ready to move forward. That her early years somehow dictated how she saw life. *I can't do this right now.*

"It's okay, I should keep my thoughts to myself."

He spooned the last of the food up and ate it quickly before rising. "I'm going to head over to Daniella and Jonah's office. Give them an update. I'll see you in the morning."

He snatched up the files and moved quickly, not exactly fleeing but needing space between them so he could think clearly. He needed time to consider her words about dark lives. It begged the question of did she really see her life as a constant battle? Was there any other way out for her where she could win? He wasn't sure how to show her how her life could be more.

Clearing his mind, he reached the door of the office and knocked sharply, aware that the newlyweds might need a moment before the door opened to admit him.

Daniella settled into the seat at her desk, files and items littering it. "David?"

"Good, you're both here. My team is following the trail of the finances and came across something odd. I wanted to pass it by you."

David slid into the chair opposite while Jonah perched on Daniella's desk as David ran through the scenario unfolding.

"We both know Celeste. She worked with me on a few projects. I can't see her involved in something like that." Daniella leaned into her words, lending them weight.

"You don't think she's the one, do you, David?" Jonah rubbed his hand over his chin and cheeks, clearly weary.

Daniella croaked, "I can't see that. I mean, she's not that kind of person." She bit her lip.

He glanced at his sister, taking a moment to consider her words. "I feel more like I'm being fed a line to keep my focus away from the real deal. It doesn't read right. No single factor raises an alarm, and yet..."

Jonah searched his face. "Then I'd say you have your answer. Maybe someone in the circle she runs in knows more. Perhaps with her assistance though, we could shed more light on the truth. Get them to illuminate the dark corners."

He frowned; hearing 'dark corners' left him feeling downright uncomfortable. He gave a nod, well aware he'd investigate that thought pattern later. "Yeah."

His answer dragged a sigh from Daniella, who narrowed her eyes as she gazed at him. "Still putting up roadblocks, is she?"

"What?" He jumped, startled.

"McNally. She's the first woman in a long time who's eluded you so thoroughly. Take your time with her, David. I like her, but I get the feeling if you push her, all that will happen is she'll respond negatively." Daniella folded her hands in her lap.

"Look, I didn't come here to talk about my love life, or lack thereof," he answered, suddenly stung.

Daniella opened her mouth and Jonah stalked to behind her seat. "Leave him alone. If it's meant to be, it will." Then Jonah leaned down and kissed his wife softly on the top of her head, leaving David feeling like a third wheel.

"Well, I'm out of here." He rose and left them to it.

CHAPTER FIVE

*E*rin spent a restless night considering the information David and the team had unearthed. When she arrived in the computer room, she'd already put together a plan. Opening the door, she was ready to start when she realized David had beaten her in.

"Oh, you're here already?" she said.

"Yeah." David nodded. "Daniella reminded me we both know Celeste. I think we should go see her. She might have some information about the people involved. "

Erin slumped onto her seat and considered David's announcement. "Really? Okay, so I guess she's sure you're of the opinion she's not involved, right?" *Could it be this simple?*

David shrugged. "I honestly don't know, but Daniella is sure it's not actually her and my gut points to the 'harmless bystander' rank."

"Do you know her and her location?"

His nod settled the sudden nervous energy that bloomed inside her. "Yeah, on the southern island. We should take my personal copter. It's going to be quicker than a vehicle and a boat. There's also less chance of being detained. I mean, so far we've seen little evidence that their critical thinking is advanced enough to plan for something like that, but we can't take any chances now."

Erin stared at David. *Personal copter?* That he spoke about that so glibly reinforced the differences between them. She put the thought away. Now she needed to concentrate on the upcoming mission.

"Right. Fine. Do you have to file a flight plan or..." She waved her hand to indicate that she was unsure what other things he may need to do under the circumstances.

"No. We should try to stay under the radar. Her family has a large estate down there, reinforced and well-guarded from what Daniella has said in the past. We will radio ahead once we're within communications distance and alert her to be ready to pick up. I'll have Daniella send a coded message too, alerting her that we're enroute. That way the guards won't be alarmed when we arrive. I've already requisitioned the fuel, and the engineers are attending to the refueling now."

She stared at him. "You've been busy," Erin said faintly.

"Grab what you need, I believe it's fairly cool down there at the moment." He turned away, and she wondered what else had happened that she didn't know about. Being kept in the dark over assignments pissed her off. *How am I supposed to know what I need to prepare?*

On the other hand, he was the senior officer so she'd follow his directions. Besides, she knew he was good at his job. He considered all aspects and didn't put people into danger if he could help it. Her mind spun, and she groaned inaudibly, checked he hadn't heard her, then reached for the Kevlar jacket she'd stashed over the back of her chair. The heavy fabric would do double duty as ballistic proof defense and keep her warm.

Erin gulped when he did the same. The skin-tight, black ballistic pants she wore molded to her hips and outlined every lump and bump. She glanced away. "Should I change?"

"Might be best," he countered. "We need to get moving quickly."

She reached into the bag under the desk, ducked into the bathroom, and slid them on in place of the combat pants she wore and returned swiftly.

"Come on." He indicated she should follow him.

They locked the lab and hurried down the hall and outside. Where she joined him in the vehicle. With a quick flick, he engaged the engine and drove through the base. At the internal connecting check-point to the base beside their military one, he stopped, showed his ID and hers, then they were waved through.

This was the first time Erin had entered the airbase, and she glanced around, her interaction with both the naval and air force bases having been minimal thus far.

He drove through the office precinct and out to the airfield. At the edge, they were once again stopped, and both required to show their IDs before they entered the restricted zone.

On the asphalt sat a small, squat bubble of clear plasglass, big enough for at least four adults. The material it was made from appeared to be a heavy metal structure and she goggled.

"Isn't that, you know, too heavy?" She pointed to the body, and he laughed.

"New generation. My uncle is an aerodynamics engineer and was using it as a test unit. It's about a third of the weight of normal plasglass and metal with a high-tensile reinforcement skin."

She must have looked lost at his answer. "Means we can fly further and quickly, safely, and it's not as heavy as it looks."

"Oh. Okay."

"Strap in. I have to talk to the engineers and commander, then we'll be on our way." He climbed from the car and she followed suit, wandering over to the craft while David met with the men in green baggies at the tail of the copter.

She peered into the tiny craft, her stomach tied in knots. She wasn't afraid he'd hurt them, just the clear panels made it seem like she was floating about the surface.

The knowledge that they'd be traveling in this machine was…*discomforting*.

He joined her after a few minutes. They climbed in, donned headsets.

"Get your belt on," he said, and she noted that for all he was moving around, clicking buttons and turning dials, there was no tell-tale rock of the machine.

"Here we go." He depressed the engine ignition point, and the doors slid shut and gave a tiny click as they locked in place. "Ready?"

She gulped as the whine of this engine started. It was unlike any she'd ever encountered, more like the starting of a car.

Looking up, she noted the blurring of the blades spinning, and a sudden greasiness invaded her belly.

David spoke into the microphone fitted into his earphones and they lifted. "You don't get flight sick, do you?" He spoke jokingly as she gripped the bar ahead of her.

She glanced to see him grinning at her. "Uh, no." At least she didn't think so.

"Good. In case you do, I have some sickness bags behind you. The trick is to focus ahead, not up or down. This should only take us an hour or so." His voice took on a soothing tone, and she nodded, looking forward into the distance as they rose.

The seat was comfortable, warm in the cool temperatures, and she silently thanked his foresight in suggesting the ballistic jacket, pleased it warded off the chill.

One time she looked down, the area they passed over was wooded with no signs of habitation, but the sensation of nausea didn't return. "It doesn't look like they're interested in the non-urbanized areas."

"No. Which makes me think that they're severely limited on troop numbers and seeking the best use of resources. If they weren't, I believe we'd see camps of them scattered even in country areas by now. I wonder if they've had to push up the timetable since we found the maturation chambers and with Clarissa."

Erin considered that. "That's an interesting theory. I mean, the children they have are still mainly first gen, right? Why risk their breeding stock to fight?"

He blinked and turned in her direction. "You're right. It doesn't make sense."

With a nod, Erin continued, "We learned with Olante that they've not got high-level strategists on side, apart from the general, and he was threatened to ensure they gained his cooperation. Not the best way to achieve the desired outcome." She pursed her lips and turned away in time to catch the glint of blue water beneath them, frothing whitecaps small sailing boats. "I've never been here before."

"Really? When this is done, we should bring the team down here for some R and R." *If we survive.* They'd all come far too close to death on more than one occasion.

How many would make it?

The children were becoming bolder, as if their natural exuberance was overtaking their training. Erin made a mental note to flick that idea past Clarissa when they got back. She understood the inner workings of a child's mind much better than she ever would.

David spoke softly into the headphones, alerting the compound of their ETA, and his lips thinned. Erin frowned. "No, we were informed that Miss Celeste would be in residence."

"Dav—"

He cut her off with a terse shake of his head. Then he growled and turned the copter onto an eastern heading.

"What's going on?" She gripped the bar before her with white-knuckled hands as the craft banked.

"She's not there. Decided to go sailing when a friend invited her earlier today. They're unsure where she is. The friends have a ketch, *Sun Spinner*, which is usually at a marina in the harbor. I want to fly over and see if it's still berthed, otherwise this was a wild-goose chase."

He exuded cold waves of fury, and she firmed her lips together. Time was precious, and currently the situation was too fraught to just accept whatever intel they received without question.

"David? We could head back to base. I've had a thought about a couple of angles we could check out."

David grunted, "Let's do the fly over first then…"

A sound and flash warned her. "David!"

Energy rippled in the air as he almost turned the copter on its side, riding the ripple. "We need to get out of here."

The copter shuddered under his hands, fighting against his commands. Sweat poured off her, fingers gripping the metal bar hard, feeling the bite in the flesh of her palms.

It felt like hours, though afterward she'd recognize it took mere minutes before they were once more flying over the water, barely skating over the surface. "Aren't we a little low?"

"Yeah." He didn't look, didn't joke, and that told Erin they were in serious danger.

A warning light flashed on the console in front of him. He grunted and twiddled a knob.

The light dimmed but didn't go out.

"Did it damage…"

"Don't know." They'd gained the land once more and headed for a heavily wooded area. "This is the most direct route to the base. I just don't know if we'll make it, Erin. I'll do my best but…" He let the words hang, increasing her terror.

"O…kay." She breathed the words, scrunching up her eyes, afraid of what she'd see if watching their flight path.

An insistent beeping filled the air, and she shuddered, inhaling deeply, and forced her eyes to open.

He swore. Loudly. "Start looking for open ground. Somewhere we can set down. There's a malfunction in the rotor systems."

She looked out the window, but all she could see were trees. Smoke puffed ahead, and she pointed it out. "Maybe that's a camp?"

"We head that way then." His skin took on a tight red visage, and she hoped he'd make it together with the ailing craft.

The gray, billowing clouds grew heavier. A thick plume rose from a fire, and an old truck with people were gathered, filling the clearing they headed for.

David swore again.

"No, wait! I don't think they're warrior children, David. Look at them. They appear older than any we've yet come across. Late teens. Besides, in the middle of nowhere?" Her guts jittered with fear. "Put it down before we fall out of the sky."

He agreed, but for all her careful protestations she unholstered her pistol and waited for someone to shoot at them.

The kids, probably in their late teens, stared at them, clearly surprised that a jet copter landed by the bonfire while they landed with a thud.

One of the teens stood and started in their direction. Erin held up the pistol for him to view.

The young man's eyes widened, and he shifted his hands into the air. She waited for the doors to unlatch then scrambled from the ailing machine.

"Where are we?" she demanded to know.

The boy flinched at her harsh tone. "Near... Near Homewoods, in the Sauvee province."

David joined her. "Can you fix what's wrong?" She chanced a quick sideway glance at him.

He shrugged. "Possibly, with the right tools and time. But that was hard flying, Erin. I need some time to rest, and it'll need to cool down before I touch anything."

Erin squinted at him, noticing the fine tremors of his hands, the glassy tinge to his green eyes. "Fine. So, what next? We can possibly camp here or—"

"Umm, ma'am?" the boy ventured. "I know someone who may be able to help, but if you need replacements, the hardware wouldn't arrive here tonight, and the light's fading fast. Besides, we've got more classmates coming to celebrate here tonight."

She glanced at the motley assembly of young adults before her. "What's happening here?"

"Graduation. But we're only a half hour from town. If we can lift that onto the truck bed, I can drive you there. We've got some mechanics who might be able to help you."

Uncertain what was the best option, she turned to David. "We can't afford to raise suspicions—"

The boy shook his head. "S'okay, my parents own a farm on the edge of town. Got a big barn. If we take it there, you can walk to the village. I'll tell you who to see and where. They'll help, I'm sure. Hey, don't I know you?"

The boy pointed at David, and he winced. "No, I doubt it."

"Yeah, I do. You're involved with the children thing. It's a topic of conversation here. People are real worried that it'll spill over to here. We're quiet. The families hereabouts mainly came after the wars. We're pacifists, man. Not looking for a war of any kind."

David shifted nervously, and she could see him tossing up options. "If we can hoist it onto the truck, we'll take the offer of assistance."

There were four teens beside Cam—their chatty guide—Erin, and David.

As she lined up to assist, David growled, "No lifting, remember?"

"But—"

"Desk duties if you don't follow orders, McNally."

She seethed as he stood firm, but stepped back as they lifted the craft to the bed of the truck. Then it was covered with oilskin and secured.

Cam scratched his head and looked at David and herself. "I haven't seen a copter like this. Was thinking about attending flight school, but the farm needs me right now. We're going to make a profit this year, first time ever. Da breeds horses and sheep, grows trees for harvesting for the big mansions. They pay real good." The boy shrugged. "But this is a beauty."

David cleared his throat. "You came here after the wars, you said. So you can't have been here that long."

"About three years. A bunch of Da's friends said they couldn't live in the cities after what they'd seen and done, so they pooled their money and bought this section. We even built a town. We've got nearly five hundred with Da's mates and all their families. We got a medic and a padre."

David cocked a brow. "And a school?"

The boy glowered, and Erin laughed at his expression. "Well, kid, I guess you've just about got everything then."

David shot her a look, and she shrugged.

"We sure could use a copter pilot." The boy shook his head. "Last year my friend Dougie, he got caught in a tree. Took three hours to get him out, then he had to drive out to the nearest emergency health center. They reckon if he'd got faster care he would have kept his leg. Now he's got a titanium one. Hates the bastard."

They climbed into the truck; it was a tight fit, and Erin almost sat on David's lap. It wasn't helping her state of mind or interest. They bounced on the uneven road until a wooden building came in view. "This is the first barn. We'll offload your copter here, and I'll drop you in town."

The other teens who'd followed in another farm vehicle piled out as they parked next to the vehicle they'd traveled in.

"But we don't have enough…" she started.

Cam shook his head. "Don't need it. Got a hoist."

The doors of the barn sat open, and the boy, Cam, drove into the darkness. He stopped in the center and killed the engine.

They climbed out and he, together with the other teens, moved to the end of the building, wound down an old-fashioned type of winch, and grabbed piles of chains from the hook beside them. "Let's get this around the body, then we can lift it."

Rattles and clanks filled the air as they climbed around and over the machine.

Time passed but the chopper lifted off the track bed and rose into the air. Erin followed the instructions and drove the vehicle out the other side and away from the barn then came back in time to hear David and Cam talking.

"If they work on it here, we can hoist it back up then put it onto a hay trailer, and the field around the shed should be big enough for you to lift off from. Yeah?" Cam said.

David nodded. "That sounds like a workable plan."

David watched, utterly fascinated with the ease the boy showed in getting the copter off his truck while Erin smoothly pulled the vehicle forward into the rapidly darkening twilight. Then the group gently lowered the transport to the ground.

Erin joined him but remained silent, and he read her uncertainty. He too was unsettled, yet this was their best hope.

"Where are your parents?" David asked.

"Oh, they're off stocking up on supplies. Lots of the olds have gone with them to Randtown, 'cause they reckon if this gets worse, we're going to need to be able to hunker down here. We're pretty much off the beaten track, but they need stuff like flour, medical supplies, and the like." The boy shrugged his meaty shoulders.

"We'll bunk down here for tonight then. If you could just get us to town, we need to communicate with our base and see who we can get out to help with the copter repairs." David pointed to the shed.

"Sure. Hop in and we'll slip by the house, grab some bedding and food for—"

"We're prepared. Can you just take us into town? We can make our own way back."

The boy glanced at him under shaggy, dirty blond hair. "Sure. It'll only take a moment or two."

Cam got them into town within five minutes, and they scrambled out of the truck. David speared Erin with a glance and a terse, "Comm back to base. No details." Then he strode after the boy, around the corner, to gain a quick survey of the spread.

The township was more like a village with a butcher, small grocery market, and hall squatting beside a postal center and emergency medical clinic and a school.

Tiny didn't really describe the buildings hidden below the canopy of the trees surrounding the town. Four cars slid by, all pick-ups like the boy—Cam—drove. They weren't new or shiny, yet he hadn't yet seen one scowl or heard a single swear word.

When David and Cam returned to Erin, they walked behind the butcher and found the mechanics garage, hidden from view. A weary-looking fuel pump sat out front, jury-rigged onto a wooden platform though it barely raised the bowser above the ground.

"Hey, Jude! I got someone here needs your help and maybe Astrid's."

A pair of shoes attached to legs protruded from below the body of another beaten up pickup, and David hunched down. "Sir? I would certainly appreciate your assistance. I've got a copter that—"

A man slid out from under the vehicle on a sliding bed. "*I know you*. You're a Villede. You bringing your troubles and those kids to our village?" The man pushed up, glowering, and for the first time David struggled with the fury the man exuded.

Before he could explain the man continued, "We don't want to fight, saw enough of that in the war. If that's what you're here for…" He waved a wrench in David's direction, the grime coating it made it appear the perfect weapon right now.

"No, sir. My partner and I were flying through when the engine was damaged. We were trying to limp home but brought it down in a clearing. Cam here helped us out. We need to fix the rotor engine, then we'll be out of your way."

He certainly hoped it would be that simple, otherwise they'd have to leave it here and find an alternative form of transport, and based on what he was seeing, it would likely be a borrowed truck. Neither comfortable nor fast. It would take them days to get back, at least if the rotor was the problem—it may be simple and they'd return home tomorrow.

The man sneered at him from beside the truck and waited as if sizing him up. "What kinda copter?"

"A retrofitted ZM-11."

"Shit! Really?" The anger seemed to melt from the man as his gaze took on a hungry look. "They're still in testing phase."

David jammed his hands into his pants and shook his head. "My uncle is the senior aerodynamics engineer. This one has a custom plasglass DM, non-standard skinning cabin, and—"

"Cam, go get Astrid. Tell her I got her something special to play with."

Erin stepped closer to him. "Astrid?"

"My partner. She was working with MaxCorp before the war, and is an engineering whiz. Now come help me load old Sally, my trusty pickup, with tools."

Erin cleared her throat, and the greasy man frowned. "She your partner or we got another unknown in our midst?"

"She's my partner, Erin McNally."

The man tightened up again, and he almost sighed. "She won't tell anyone our location, if that's your concern."

"You'd be trackable," he grumbled, and David shook his head.

"We've got location tracking disablers installed on all our comms devices and a specially encrypted comm program," Erin offered.

"Huh."

The man shoved a pile of rags into his hands and a red-haired woman entered. "Cam said you've got toys to play with?"

"A retrofitted ZM-11," Jude muttered.

"Don't you try to fool me, you canny bastard. The ZM's are all in testing phase." The woman—Astrid, he guessed—glowered at Jude, then himself and Erin while Cam jittered in the doorway.

"These two here reckon they've got one over at Cam's barn. That it's got a compromised rotor motor. We'll go over, and if there is one, we need to get it fixed."

David spoke quietly. "We have to get back to base ASAP."

"If it's not one of those, you'll hear about it, young man." With lightning speed Astrid snapped a set of keys from the pegboard by the door. "Got the repairs finished?"

The grimy man groaned. "One more nut and we're done."

"Then get under there, so we can get out to the barn."

He muttered, crawled beneath the vehicle, and rattled around before re-emerging. "Done. Drop the hoist and we'll be on our way."

Astrid touched a button, the vehicle slid down, and they piled in after Astrid dismissed Cam with a casual, "You got things to do, haven't you, Cam?"

It was a good thing it was an extended cab, so there was seating for the four of them, he thought as they bounced back in the direction of the barn.

"He's a good boy is Cam. Wants to learn to fly, but hasn't got the money or connections. Reckon it comes from watching Dougie struggle. They're best mates, and it's a drawback to our lifestyle. We choose not to have all the modern conveniences but..." Astrid shrugged. "We decided after the wars we couldn't do that again. Living cheek-by-jowl isn't something we're able to deal with. We need space. And we couldn't live a normal lifestyle, because most of us have our issues. This way we have space, our families have a future, and we live in peace."

"Sounds like a lifestyle many would want," Erin said in a low voice.

"Some." Astrid cleared her throat. "Others just want to make life difficult for everyone, and we've all been under the thumb long enough. Can't stand asswads like those controlling the children. Who's behind all that anyway?" Her direct words meant he couldn't fudge his answer.

"I can't disclose what we know, I'm sorry, Astrid. Our investigations have put us in the position that what we have gleaned must remain confidential."

"Huh, he's a smooth talker this man of yours. What'd you say your name was?"

Erin shifted beside him in the seat, her face burning. "He's not... We're not together, if you get my meaning. We're just co-workers." She fumbled her words, leaving Astrid snorting and him wishing her answers weren't true.

CHAPTER SIX

hey'd spent several hours working on the copter. Upon seeing it, Astrid had exclaimed with excitement, "You told the truth. They're supposed to just be conceptual, and the weight!" The woman ran her hands over the shell, ohhing and ahhing with excitement.

David had answered her questions, and Erin watched on, having retrieved the bedding sacks and emergency supplies from the tiny space behind their seats.

Now the couple had left, promising to return in the morning to help fix the last issues. "You can't tell anyone we're here or what you've seen," David pressed.

"Asswad," muttered Astrid while Jude muttered, "I know the drill. Need to know and all that."

Even so, Erin stashed her tiny laser pistol into the back of her ballistic pants, just in case someone unfriendly found them.

"Help me with the bed," she grunted, having laid the emergency sacks out, and he knelt on the ground.

"They just a self-inflater?"

"Yeah, just pull the end and turn it clockwise. That autoprimes the pump," she answered.

The night air crept in, and even with the barn doors closed, jackets donned, and snuggled down in the beds it was cool. The MRE's—Meals Ready to Eat—were as flavorless as she remembered, but they filled the gnawing pit in her belly.

Earlier Cam had showed them the location of the long-drop toilet, for which Erin was grateful. While it wasn't exactly high on her list of things to experience, at least it had three walls a roof and door. *An improvement on the great outdoors.*

Erin lay back, checking out the view above, wondering how long it would take to doze off.

"Tell me about yourself, Erin." David's query surprised her.

His words had her thinking back over her life, and her eyes stung with unshed tears. She blinked furiously, banishing them. "There isn't much to tell. I was abandoned at the hospital where I was born. My mother was likely fifteen according to the official reports, when I popped out. One thing I know categorically is she never gave her real name. I was popped out then off she went. I have no idea who my father is. Don't really care. I was in foster care after a couple of attempts at adoption and placement. Tried a couple of foster families, but we didn't take to each other, so I went back to the home. I graduated and moved on. Tried to join the military, and here I am." It was barebones and very few knew the intricacies of what came before. The hurt and abandonment. The layers of protection she'd built around herself.

"Wasn't much of a childhood." He touched a hand to her shoulder for an instant. The action unbalancing her with the support he clearly offered.

"It was okay. I mean, sure, I don't have a flesh and blood family, but I also don't have that miserable family politics a lot of others have either. I choose who I want to know, where I go. My days are my own."

"But what about birthdays and holidays?"

"Aren't they kind of over-rated? People go out, spend all that money, get drunk, and have to see Great-Aunt Gertie who hates you anyway."

David laughed, clearly at a loss to understand her reasoning from the sound of it. "Sometimes, but it's better to be festive with the people you love around you. To be part of something bigger than yourself."

"Maybe, but I've been doing this long enough to know I don't have to have it to feel fulfilled, you know? I spend *Ramustas* at home usually, watching vids or painting. I like the solitude, and usually the apartments around are empty so I can turn it up loud, throw popped corn at the screen, and stuff like that."

"It's almost *Ramustas* now. What will you do?"

She sighed, knowing this year there'd be no way to ignore it. "I usually ask for duty so someone with a family can spend it with them. It's about kids and families. I guess there'll be a meal in the mess. That'll be nice. The rest of the day, I'll probably sack out. Read a book. Keep busy."

"Spend it with us. Daniella, Jonah, Clarissa, Michael, and the baby."

He must have almost surprised himself with that question, but she smiled, appreciating the care and thought in his invitation. "Maybe not. Not that I don't like your family. They're great, but... I'd just feel like you're being kind..." She floundered for the right words so he wouldn't have to get angry that she thought he was pitying her. *Which, no doubt he is.*

"No, really, Erin. I'd love for you to join us."

She winced, and her mind tried to compute the best way to decline. "How about we just wait and see? Life depends on so many things right now."

Erin rolled to her side, hoping he'd take the hint, but the rasp of bedding on the ground, followed by the touch of his hand again, snaking around her shoulders, pulling her in to his embrace. "I mean it."

Warmth filled her, insidiously drugging her and grinding on her mind. He might mean it, but she wasn't sure she could handle it. Erin lay still, waited for the emotion to pass, and drifted off to sleep.

D avid waited for the slow, rhythmic breathing that told him Erin had finally given in and slumbered. "Why? Why do you pull away? What is it that makes you feel that you need to keep a wall between us?"

She'd had a rough start, true, but it didn't explain the way she stayed apart from others. The genuine sense of disconnection from life and others.

Getting to the bottom on that might give him a foothold in her heart, though not nearly enough; it might be a starting point.

The incident where she'd been injured guarding Daniella had come far too close to wiping her from life, and that he couldn't tolerate. He'd realized then that he'd been squandering his chances, and that knowledge gnawed at him for the last several weeks.

Today, when he'd talked with Cam, Astrid, and Jude he'd watched her. She'd been friendly and yet that air of 'don't touch me' had remained intact and he'd wanted to crash through it.

Too much too soon, he reminded himself, though he kept his arm around her. It took a long time before he too slept.

CHAPTER SEVEN

*D*awn brought with it wakefulness and the roar of an engine. Erin scooted from the bed and pulled the tiny toggle before waking David. He stashed the bedding while she ran for the toilet then greeted Astrid and Jude who'd brought with them something that smelled mouthwateringly delicious.

"Since we gathered you only had MREs we brought breakfast muffins. This one is chicken and corn. The other is bacon and sundried tomatoes." The woman passed a small basket filled with the food into her arms. "And coffee, since the army and every service we've ever had anything to do with lived on that too."

The muffins, warm from the oven, and the travel mugs would be an excellent start to the day, and the four settled onto hay bales. "Astrid, how long have you been here?" Erin bit into the baked item and moaned at the tastes that exploded on her tongue.

The woman eyed her speculatively. "We've been here since Cam's Da, Patrick, put the plan forward. There were five families initially that pooled to purchase land, but since then we've grown to nineteen. Why? You interested in joining us?"

Erin choked on a crumb at the woman's question. "No! Just trying to work out why you'd come to somewhere like this."

Astrid gazed at her, cold blue eyes steady. "We fought battles where men and women killed each other face-to-face. Where the blood and stench became the only thing we knew we could expect. We watched the life drain from girls and boys barely old enough to comprehend what we were all fighting for. It stays with you, the kids. The death. The smells. Eats at you so that one day you reach the point where you can't fight anymore. Where being around people who don't understand becomes just as dangerous as the battlefield."

Astrid inhaled and then released the oxygen with a whoosh.

"We knew, when we came here, that we were hiding from the world. Accepted that, because we did what was necessary to save the citizens from a world of slavery and corruption, but the cost to ourselves was almost the loss of our souls. We've given all we could, Erin. Now we need to heal. We needed to reconnect with nature and life and be free. That's why we came here. To be truly able to live our lives and to become, if not the people we were before, then the people we now are."

Erin pondered the words. "Is it working for you?"

Astrid smiled, an uptick of her lips. "Yes and no. Hiding away doesn't solve anything, but to be honest, the peace and tranquility have allowed most of us to come to terms with what we've done."

She finished her muffin. "That was really good. I haven't had anything like that in a long time."

Astrid smiled at her. "Maybe when you're done, you'll come back here and visit. But for now, let's take a look at this copter."

The work was companionable, the two men and Astrid conferring while Erin remained watchful. By mid-morning, the rotor fully repaired, they ferried the copter onto the hay trailer and into the open air. David and Erin climbed inside, and Astrid pushed another bundle of muffins into her hands. "For the journey."

Once Astrid and Jude retreated to the barn, David ran through the pre-flight checks, engaged the engine, and up they rose. Erin chanced a final look down at the barn before it disappeared from sight.

D avid wasn't sure what Astrid had said to Erin that put such an introspective look on her face, but she'd been quiet during the flight and subsequent drive back to their base. She'd excused herself at the lines and scurried up the steps as he watched. Something had changed, some quality about her, indefinable yet obvious.

He scratched his head and headed for the computer lab they'd set up at the clinic. Sevres and Fairburn were there as was Maylin. "You made it back."

He snorted. "Just a small detour first."

Fairburn snorted. Sevres simply raised an eyebrow, shrugged, and returned to his work. "What did you learn while I was away?"

"Celeste and her friend Sorrington—yes, the one Fairburn was chasing down—decided on the spur of the moment to go for a sail on his yacht, the *Sun Spinner*. They're expected to be gone for another couple of days, meaning there wouldn't be any benefit in trying to track her down for another couple of days. The timing is convenient, I agree."

David frowned at Maylin, wondering just how far she could dig into the system without alerting PolSearch. He asked and she grinned.

"Let's see, shall we?" Maylin tugged the keyboard closer after settling into the chair, and within moments she was diving beneath the surface of the heavily encoded system. "See, this will allow me to circumvent the trace system. Most coders build back doors into their programs, allowing them to make corrections and to override parts of the code. I happened to know one of the people working on building the new PolSearch security modules. They showed me this portal."

Maylin's fingers flew now, tapping and turning off aspects of the system which would grant her access to secure documents and files.

"And there you have it," she said. "Sorrington's background, links to his current financial documentation, and even his religious and political connections."

David frowned. "Say that again."

Maylin chortled, no doubt surprised at his demand. "I've got access to current financials—"

Squeezing his eyes shut, David pinched the bridge of his nose as the thought bloomed. "Not that."

"His current political affiliations?"

"No, Maylin. His religious affiliations. Get me what you have." The idea chewed at him, teeth sinking deeply into his psyche. *Religion.* They'd ignored anything to do with that, because the majority of people had eschewed any form of belief system these days. It could be a wild-goose chase, but the alarm blaring in his head wouldn't be ignored.

David stalked to the coffee machine and poured one for himself and another for Erin as she entered the room, having changed out of the wrinkled clothing and Kevlar jacket, replacing them with clothing less battle ready but nevertheless form-fitting. He held the cup out to her, and she accepted it in silence.

She looked around the room, eyes focusing on Maylin, then turned back to him "What's going on?"

"I had a thought, and Maylin is following up on it. What if we've been attacking this from the wrong direction? I mean, we have points of interest for many of our players, but someone is pulling the strings. Someone with clout and resources."

Erin's nose wrinkled. "I know that, but you've got something vastly different in your sights, don't you?"

"You don't believe in any form of religion, yet you celebrate *Ramustas*, right?"

She jerked as if he'd hit her, but David raised his hand before she could argue. "No, just listen. You think it's just about the kids and families, but others with deeper beliefs would—"

She blinked once, the tightness of her facial features softening. "They'd be looking for some kind of religious meaning. That's the way you're going?" Disbelief dripped from her words. "No one believes in that hocus-pocus religion crap these days."

David shrugged. "As a kid, my parents made sure Michael, Daniella, and I attended the Monastery for religious interpretation classes."

Erin stared, eyes wide open, her mouth dropping at his words.

"There are many who believe in the teachings of *Rumasa*. My parents among them. There are those who believe we are too lax in the way we celebrate the religion. Some have moved their teachings underground and become fundamentalist in their practice. It's been like that for time immemorial. People taking their beliefs to the extreme." David got up and paced around the seat as he spoke. "What if that's what the deal is here? What if we need to stop looking at it from a purely financial and political standpoint and add in a personal belief or beliefs that absolves them from responsibility for the way they achieve the outcome."

Erin shook her head. "You're reaching, David. Who in their right mind would allow some antiquated belief system to run their decision making?"

He sighed. "You're so damned linear at times, Erin. Stop thinking in terms of A plus B equals C. Just for a moment, suspend your disbelief and join the dots."

Erin shrugged. "I guess it's possible."

David could tell she wasn't sold on his suggestion, but she nodded. "Okay then, what next?"

"Maylin is already investigating their religious affiliations. If they have one."

They waited as Maylin dove deeper, and clenched their hands when the woman heaved a sigh. "So, I have what you're looking for... Well, kind of. Yes, they are all affiliated to a religious doctrine. But while some follow *Rumasa*, we have some Christians and even *Asatru*. There is no one belief system. I'm sorry, David." Maylin stood up and shrugged.

David inhaled, released the tension in his shoulders, and gazed into the coffee cup. "I was so hopeful."

Erin slid her hand over his, the prickle of awareness at her closeness difficult to suppress. "It's okay. We'll find something. There has to be a hint somewhere. They all fit in somehow. We just have to find the key."

For the first time, he allowed his frustration at the inability to find the connection bubble to the surface. "Perhaps, but at the rate we're going it will be too late."

Frustrated, David tugged away, slammed the coffee on the bench, and left the room.

E rin watched David leave. She understood his frustration, but the thought that he'd believe religion might be the reason for all this? She shook her head. "No one believes in that anymore."

Behind her the pad of feet startled her, so she jerked. "Some do. He does obviously. But his frustration is palpable, Erin. We need to find the key...and so far no one has been able to give it to us. Has Liv given you any ideas? Perhaps she might be able to shed light on what lies at the heart of this."

Maylin's words crashed into her mind. Liv. She might know something. Perhaps it was time to see the child, since she'd been moved to the open ward, her injuries requiring special care. She vaguely remembered someone saying she'd remain there until such time as Daniella and Jonah had settled into the cottage being set up for their use.

"That's a great thought. I'll go see her now. Thanks for your help, Maylin."

Erin spun and left the room, well aware that the child might not be able to shed any further light onto the conundrum that plagued them all. *Don't go discounting before you can be sure.*

Marching across the compound, she pondered the thoughts, until her communicator blared. "McNally," she answered.

"Just the person I need." *Jonah.*

"What's up?"

"Are you in earshot of anyone?" he asked.

She glanced around and responded that she was alone.

"Good I've got a mission. Top secret for you. Meet me at Daniella's office as quickly as you can."

His tone and words piqued her interest, so she veered in that direction, frowning when

David came into view. *Dammit. If he sees me, he'll want to know why I'm here. Jonah won't like that.* She ducked behind the building and waited before peering around the corner. He was gone, and heaving a sigh of relief, she scurried to the door. The handle moved, and once the way was open, she stepped into the hall, pleased David wasn't there either, since she didn't know where he'd gone. Several steps took her to the door to Jonah's office, and she knocked.

The door opened and there stood David. *Oh no!*

"Come in, McNally."

Gritting her teeth, she followed Jonah's curt instructions and waited.

"Now that you're both here, I have a mission for you. Both of you. It seems Celeste Landry is missing. She was last seen aboard the yacht, *Sun Spinner*, with Draven Sorrington. You need to find her before it's too late."

Erin scowled. "He's probably already—"

Jonah shook his head. "No. She contacted Daniella this morning, raising the alarm. She slipped away overnight, because Sorrington had scared her. Enough that she was willing to jump ship with an inflatable dingy, some water and her communicator. Time is of the essence, and I believe she may be able to give us the connection we're looking for. You're cleared to use the copter and all speed. I've arranged a boat out of the harbor for cover. Get moving and find her before anyone else does."

"But Jonah, what about the investigation into the funds?" An itch started on the back of her neck. Search and rescues weren't something she was good at, let alone those that included flying and water.

"Sevres, Fairburn, Maylin, and I will continue that side of the investigation. Finding Celeste is priority though. She contacted us specifically because she said she'd overheard something about the warrior children and yours and David's investigation was a threat. She said there's more and it runs deep, but her communicator battery is running low. We'll keep working from our side, but I need you two out there, finding her, before they do. I need you on this now."

With no time to waste they were quickly bundled out of the office, feet pounding across the asphalt toward their accommodation units. "I need to grab some cold weather clothes, particularly in case we get wet."

He grunted something unintelligible, and Erin glanced at him. "What's your problem?"

"It's taking too many twists. Nothing about this investigation makes sense. We have so little to go on."

"Well, maybe this is the link we need so we can work out what comes next."

"I'll meet you back here in ten. We can arrange the copter to be ready on our way over to the airbase." Then David turned and left her to it, watching him retreat.

Without a further sound, Erin headed for her room, pulled open the door, and stepped inside, only to be shocked to see Liv sitting on her bed and not in the infirmary where she was supposed to be.

"Hope you don't mind. I let myself in. There's some chatter about your mission, and I couldn't help but overhear it, so when I got to the lab and they said you weren't there, this seemed the next obvious place to look for you."

Erin stared at the girl. "I'm in a hurry, Liv. Talk while I pack, but unless you have something useful to tell me, then I'm going to have to cut you short, okay?"

She turned, pulled a backpack from under the bed, and flung open the wardrobe, hunting for fresh underwear, pants, longer sleeve shirts, and spare boots.

"Where you going?"

Erin didn't turn to look at the girl, simply set about dragging out the clothes she needed. "On a mission, and I don't know where."

"Huh! Well, you're looking for a connection between Colvert, Olante, and Corvino, right?" Liv's words stopped Erin in her tracks.

"What?"

"I heard the names," the girl muttered. Erin grabbed the boots by the bed, already shucking the lighter lofa shoe she'd been wearing as Liv continued, "You're looking for the financial backer, right? Oh, it comes through from more than four locations, yeah?"

Now Erin stopped, spun back to stare at the girl. "What did you just say?"

"Oh, they had us girls assist in the office space. Said that training us to be useful while growing the next generation was another part of our task. I had a better head for numbers than a lot of others, so they started training me in the financial side of things. I saw some of the income strands. The ones from the World Bank were the smallest amounts, but the same person handled them."

"Who?"

"Stollington? Sorrington? Something like that. He's the go-between, according to some of the communications I saw, okay?"

Erin swiped her hand over her brow, her mind thinking in rapid fire. "So, you saw the name Draven Sorrington?"

"No, not a guy... Elina Sorrington or something like that was the signatory. I don't know a Draven. It's not a name I saw."

Biting her lip, Erin considered the girl's words. "Okay. Get yourself back to the medical center. They'll be worried about where you are. I'm heading out and can't get you back there right now. Make sure you tag either the senator or Jonah when you get back. Tell them what you told me, okay? Now go." She ushered the girl to the door.

Liv scowled. "So that's all the thanks I get? I've given up everything for you lot. I at least deserve—"

"Liv, I have a life depending on me right now." Some of the worry and concern bled into her words because the girl blinked at her. "I'll come see you when I get back."

The girl left Erin staring at the half-packed bag in her hand, then she stumbled to the bathroom, found toothbrush, paste, and a hairbrush and changed into the warmer clothes she knew were necessary. If she was missing anything...well, she'd do without it. By the time she was downstairs, Erin was winded from rushing.

David was staring pointedly at his watch.

Erin climbed into the waiting vehicle, puffing. "I have a good explanation. I'll tell you everything in the car."

Contacting the flight prep team from the vehicle cut down the amount of time they'd have to wait. They were flying light. Only a small bag each, renewed rations in the emergency pack, and the tiny jump seat cleared for Celeste meant they'd still have more than twenty hours flight time worth of fuel in the tanks.

"So, you want to hear what I have to tell you?" The asperity in Erin's voice washed over David.

"Yes, of course."

"I got upstairs, and Liv was there. Waiting for me. She'd overheard some of the conversations we'd had. She said she'd spent some time in the finances of the children's headquarters. Said she knew of Elina Sorrington or something like that, who I guess is either a sister or mother to our friend Draven. I'm just about to put a call through to Jonah to request the ID, but Liv was adamant."

The back of David's head itched. The information would help, but it was more than timely, it ranked up there with a huge coincidence. Something he didn't hold with. "How did she know about Sorrington?"

"Claims she overheard us."

His concern deepened. "She overheard us? That's what she said?"

Erin nodded. "She was definite about that. Said she'd seen communiques with that name. I didn't recognize it…"

"Tell Jonah only the necessary for now, Erin. Ask him to hold off on any action based on what she says. It feels off to me, and I don't want to send them off on a wild-goose chase. We've had a few of them already."

"David, I know your angry that—"

"I need time to consider what she told us, Erin. Please, just trust me?" He turned into the airfield and cut the engine, and his gaze connected with Erin's. "Please."

"I always trust you, David. You've never done me wrong, and I trust your instincts. Implicitly. The thing is I sent her to Jonah and Daniella. I'm sorry if that's messing with what you think."

He could tell she meant it, and it made him want to reach out to her, to tug her close and kiss her lips.

Instead he turned away and motioned for her to follow him airside, where the copter waited, several people hurrying to prepare it for their use. "Load the bags into the back. I'll be with you in a moment."

She gave a silent nod, and he glimpsed her following his instructions as he once again took control of the tiny craft.

"We've completed the pre-flight checks for you. She's fueled and ready to go. Will you be logging a flight plan?" The earnest engineer handed over the clipboard, and David ran his eyes over the list then double-checked everything. The first thing he'd learned as a pilot was the best person to rely on to ensure the safety of your craft was yourself.

Once he climbed into the cockpit and fired the engine, Erin had finished the call she'd made from her communicator. "They checked on Eliana Sorrington and can't find her at all on PolSearch." She rubbed an absent finger over the bridge of her nose.

"That's odd." His gaze moved over the equipment while his mind considered what she'd just told him.

"It is. It's almost as if she never existed, which is strange."

"You said Liv saw the dockets, the signatures, right? Anyway, we need to get moving. Hold tight." David pushed the controls, the copter rising into the air, then he dropped the nose slightly and accelerated.

"Umm, is it okay to fly like this?" Erin scrunched back in her seat, her face white.

"Yeah. I'm just accelerating more quickly than usual. It's all good. But why don't you talk to me? Ask me anything you want." He hoped that by combining her natural curiosity about life and keeping her mind occupied, they'd be able to pass the time more swiftly for him. The tilt at the front of the copter—pitching the nose down—was slight but would allow them to speed up and he'd already ascertained she wasn't a comfortable flyer.

"Okay. How long have you been flying?"

He chuckled. "I started when I was eighteen. My Uncle Ran, as you know, is an aerospace engineer. He was a flight instructor in the forces until he retired. Said he couldn't face combat flights anymore. He went commercial at that point. Took me on as his first student. He was co-opted soon after to work on the new generation copters, but by then I was hooked. So, when Uncle Ran needed someone to test this baby, I jumped at the chance. With the political instability it's come in useful for work."

"Oh. You're close, right? Your family?" Erin waved her hands.

He shrugged, his gaze scanning the horizon. "I guess. Ran is my mother's brother. Dad was an only child, so we spent a lot of time with our cousins. Mike, Daniella, and I spent summers with them, and they'd spend winters with us."

Now Erin went silent, and he glanced in her direction. She'd finally lost the white- knuckled grip on the bar ahead of her. Instead, she'd dragged on her dark glasses.

He let her be, knowing that the flight and the task ahead of them were big enough. He'd made some headway, and he'd take what he'd managed to achieve as a sign that he was on the right track.

CHAPTER EIGHT

*A*t some point, Erin mused, she must have fell asleep, because as her eyes opened, they'd reached the sandy expanse and the flash of blue water extended beyond the front of the copter.

"With us again?" Amusement colored David's tone, and she almost squeaked with embarrassment.

"Uh, how long was I out?" She pushed the glasses up over her hair, a little embarrassed that she'd slept, and caught sight of his grin.

"Not that long."

"Okay, so where are we, and how long until we reach the location of Celeste?"

"Her position was about two nautical miles from here. She knows the area well and was able to tell us pretty closely the location and sent us some photos before her comm system went offline. I'm going to have to quick stop. It's tricky. I've got to wash off the speed, hover and drop down if there are things in the way. Not my preferred landing type, but it's all we'll have."

"O-kay." The way he spoke told her more about the danger than he probably realized. "We'll be able to take off easily?"

"Yeah."

"Why is it different to what we did—"

He turned. "I'll explain later. Once we're safely back at the base, okay?"

She nodded and, now silenced, waited for him to give further instructions.

"In the box behind your seat there are binocs. Grab them out. I need you to be on the lookout for a small island in a group of five. They're called the 'Five Brides'. We need to find the middle one. It's got a cave where she's hidden the dingy and is hiding out. Once we fly over, he'll know and send backup, so we'll have to move quickly and be decisive." He thrust a small communicator at her. "You'll find her listed under 'B' for 'Buffy', so dial and tell her what to look out for."

'B' for 'Buffy'. Erin wasn't sure she liked how close and friendly this all sounded. *And why is that, hmm? You've avoided him and any kind of connection studiously. Now you're what... Jealous?*

She snatched up the binocs, refusing to consider the situation any further. They flew along the coastline, keeping it on the pilot's side as she glanced out the window.

The expanse of blue glowed like a sapphire, but no small islands caught her attention. "I can't see anything."

"All right then, we move further into the channel. I'll fly back to our starting position, and you can check again."

She nodded, realizing he needed some silence, the only sound the thudding of the blades and the engine cutting through the air. They flew swiftly, the nose once again slightly dipped, then he banked and turned the copter into a tight turn, realigning them. This time the expanse of blue on both sides increased her nausea, which she controlled with some difficulty.

"Okay, beginning the pass again."

She raised the binocs and peered through. "Hang on, what's that?" She pointed into the far distance at a speck of color against the shine of the water.

"Let's go find out."

He maneuvered, changed his heading, and powered forward, over the top of a large yacht. "Dammit!"

"What?"

"That super yacht down there? It looks like the *Sun Spinner*."

"Okay. Clearly we need to find her quickly and get out of here," Erin murmured.

They checked the small islands, counted five, and picked the central one out. She dialed 'B' for 'Buffy' and the call was answered with, "David, it took you a long time to find me."

Erin held up the unit. "Yes, longer than I wanted. Stay in the cave until I land, then run like the hounds of hell are after you. He's not that far away and we're running short on time to get off the island."

She tapped the communicator off and waited, hands clutching the bar again as he washed off speed, sand whipping around them as he hovered.

Erin knew he'd said the landing would be tricky, but he just looked cool and fresh, like he did this every day. She bit her lip and held it there, even though the tender skin stung.

They landed with a tiny thud. Sand flew into the air and Erin watched him wait until the blades stopped spinning, then he tugged off his belt and shoved the door open wide. A tiny whirlwind of blond hair with a small, lithe body, encased in a figure-hugging white and gold swimsuit, came sprinting up the hill.

He pulled his seat back, shoved the woman in, then clambered back in, closing the door and once again firing the engine. "Get your belt on, then scrunch down. We don't want them to see you until we're past them!"

David had the copter up, and the nose dipped again as they flew over a tiny speed boat, three people crowded inside. "Just missed them!"

Pings of sound echoed, 'Buffy' cowered and slapped her hands to her head, and David grimaced. "We've been hit. I don't think it's anything serious though. Erin?"

"I'm good."

"Celeste?"

"Uhh no. Not so good really. I, um, think I'm hit."

"Erin?"

She threw off the belt and turned in the seat, hissing at the red staining the other woman's swimsuit. Erin dug into the emergency supplies, searching for the first aid kit, and thanked the training in field triage. "Turn toward me."

The woman did, slowly unclasping her seatbelt with shaky hands.

Erin inspected the wound site. "I think we should be good to reach home, but I'm going to have to apply a field dressing as best I can. I'm going to start by cutting your swimsuit then will pad the wound site. It's going to hurt, but will compress the wound and slow the bleeding."

It was uncomfortable and slow, hanging over the seat, the way it pushed into her still healing wound site, but the woman wasn't going to bleed out, at least not on her watch.

Celeste yowled as she shoved the packing at her, applied firm pressure. "Hold that. Hard," Erin barked as the woman's hands flailed ineffectively.

"It hurts." Celeste employed a plaintive voice, and it took all Erin's efforts to control the eye roll.

"Yeah, it does, but I need pressure on the wound, okay?"

"You don't know how much it hurts—"

Erin smothered the words that came to her lips as David called out, "She does. She was injured just a couple of weeks ago. Nearly died from wounds like yours."

The woman's eyes squeezed shut. "Can you give me something for the pain?"

"No. I don't carry those kinds of things in my kit. This is the best I can do right now." She gave instructions, watched as the woman settled herself against the corner of the copter, and climbed back into position, which was difficult in the cramped conditions. "How quickly can we make it home?"

David's lips thinned. "I'll push as hard as I can. Maybe an hour? That's from here."

They'd already crossed the white sandy area and were quickly approaching the tree line beyond. Somewhere down there was Cam, Astrid, and Jude, who'd moved to escape this kind of situation.

"How's the copter?"

"She'll keep flying."

Erin just hoped Celeste would make it that long. Her skin was taking on a decidedly pasty whiteness. It could be shock, or it could be something far worse, and she couldn't get close enough to tell and inspect the wound site. They'd just have to hold on.

"Celeste?"

"Hmm?" It was a groan of pain and Erin frowned.

"Uh, what can you tell be about Draven Sorrington?"

"Dav? He's a friend. I went to school with him." Celeste shifted in the seat, and Erin reached out, trying to encourage her to stay as still as possible.

"Does he have a sister? Cousins? Anyone you know who's named Elina?"

"Eliana? No... Not that I know of. Our families have been friends for a long time. Mama didn't mention anyone. She's a cousin, you know. Distant."

Erin rubbed at her wound site, feeling the burn of memory. "Okay. You're sure?"

"No... Not sure. Need to ask mama." Celeste opened her eyes and Erin's concern rose another notch at the glassiness.

"David, we're going to need to detour. Get me to Cam's. We need a medic now."

"We'll be drawing them into the area if we do that."

"And if we don't, we could lose her. I can't check her pulse, but she's glassy and pasty. It could be shock, David. We need down as quickly as we can."

He banked, Celeste gasped, and Erin swore. Their descent this time was gradual, gentle even so that they landed with barely the insult of a nudge.

Erin threw off her belt and shoved the door open before the blades ceased spinning, adrenaline spiking as she ran to the other side. David was out, shoving his seat out of the way and lifting the woman over the seat. "Get her on the grass, I need to inspect the injury now. Then get hold of Astrid or Jude. We need the medic here."

Throwing herself on the ground, Erin tore at the hastily applied bandages and padding.

"Shit!" It was definitely worse, with the heat surrounding the tissue, some obvious distension which was spongy to her touch. "I think she's got some internal bleeding I missed in the cabin."

David headed off down the road. There wasn't much else Erin could do, so she repacked the site and kept pressure on the wound while she waited for David to return.

Upon his return, David was puffing and panting. "They're bringing the medic. He's going to stabilize, then we'll try and fly out of here. The longer we're here, the greater the danger to this community."

"I agree." She also remembered Cam's words about his friend, Dougie. "I just hope Cam doesn't see us."

That was a faint hope as the sound of a pickup truck echoed. Erin groaned. "Head him off, will you?"

Another sound, this time a throatier pitch, told her Astrid or Jude were there. A woman in her late thirties climbed from the back of the extra cab with a big metal box in her hands.

"Let me see," the woman bellowed, and Erin moved aside as the woman barged over. Erin stretched her aching muscles while hovering in the general vicinity.

The 'hmm's and 'okay's didn't shed any light, but Erin could afford to be patient. For Celeste to survive, they needed the expert help this woman could offer.

The medic dug deep into her carryall and produced an IV solution and got it running, setting Astrid, David, and Jude to attaching a customized, retrofitted pallet to the running board of the copter's skids.

"Is that the best we can do?" Erin queried.

"They used to do it, long ago, when transporting combatants from battlefields," David offered.

Erin subsided, aware Celeste wouldn't be going anywhere during the flight, given the way she was trussed up. A plasglass bubble would cocoon Celeste and keep her warm during their flight.

"The strapping will keep her immobilized," the medic explained as they set about fitting all the parts together. "There's nothing new in the world, you know? This system still works today."

Within twenty minutes the woman gave an, "Okay, I've stabilized her. You'll need to have an ambulance and surgical team on standby, but she'll survive the flight now."

David swiped an unsteady hand over his brow. "My brother is a surgeon. He'll be ready to receive her as soon as we arrive."

"Good. I'd appreciate an update as soon as you have her sorted at your location." The medic shook David's hand then stepped back.

Erin shook her head. "I wish we could, but to do that would bring your location under scrutiny."

"Ahh. Like that, is it? I was in the military and understand. When you can, let me know."

With all the safeguards in place, Erin and David took up their spots in the craft before he started the engines.

"This is going to be rough and ready," he offered, and Erin understood.

The flight was quick and silent, every few minutes Erin would check the stats fed from the unit containing Celeste to the communicator in her hands. Her vital signs remained within the parameters the medic had given her, and before long they'd once more arrived back at base, the small ambulance waiting and Michael hovering by the side of the unit.

David cradled his wine glass, gazing at the ruby liquid. "You know, I never realized you had combat medical training."

Erin laughed. "It's basic as you saw. Enough to gain an idea of the worst wounds, some triage skills, but that's about my limit. I just knew she needed the kind of help I couldn't give."

"Don't undersell yourself, Erin. You do that all the time." He slid the glass to the table top, pleased the bar was empty except for them.

No one would interrupt their conversation and he needed time alone with this woman, so they could get to know each other better. The conversation in the copter today had confirmed that neither understood or knew each other as well as they should.

"What do you mean?"

Inhibitions fled and he reached out, cupped her cheek, and was surprised that this time she didn't flinch away, though her gaze widened.

"You diminish your skills. *Just some triage skills*, you said. Without you doing what you did, she would have died. You saved her today by knowing what to look for. The same as other things. I know you're capable, in fact more than capable, in hand-to-hand. Your investigative skills are incredibly strong, and your empathy astounds me. But not once have I ever heard you say you're good at something."

"Yes, I have. More than once. I'm excellent in the field." Erin opened her mouth as if to say something more, then closed it again. Not for the first time, she wet her lips so they shone a dark pink in the half-light.

It was too much, the temptation far too great, and he slowly lowered his mouth to hers. "Erin, stop me now if you don't want this."

She shivered, closed her eyes, and angled upward to accept the kiss.

He kept it light, a glance, yet the sweet warmth of her breath caressed his skin, set the butterflies to wing in his belly and the deep-seated hunger roaring.

She placed her fingers over his hand, slid them up his wrist so that they tangled in his hair, anchoring him close to her.

The thudding of his heart, a rapid tattoo, increased, and he pulled away. He didn't want her to feel crowded or forced in any way.

It took every ounce of willpower for him to step back, and Erin sighed.

He smiled, satisfied she needed the touch as much as he did. "Slow steps, Erin. You need to be as comfortable with this as I am." He rested a forehead again hers for a moment then backed away.

Her eyes had closed at some time during the kiss, and reopening them seemed to take forever. The passion on her face seared him, burning him with the intensity.

"I've been thinking about it. A lot." She groaned, and he sighed at the confusion that flashed over her face. "More than I should have. I don't want to fight it any longer, David."

Excitement skittered, feeding every nerve in his body. The excitement, a rush of adrenaline threatened to overwhelm him.

David closed his eyes, tamping down on the feeling, needing to settle his emotions, so he could act on what she promised, while he stayed true to his words. It was a tussle, hard fought and even with the best of intentions, he feared, a promise he'd struggle to keep, his body clamoring for hers.

"I... Erin, you're so damned beautiful, inside and out." He spoke in a rush, needing her to understand the depths of the emotions that bubbled below the surface, but even more so, to understand he'd slow it down. That he feared the repercussions of another misstep. "More than I ever dreamed of in a woman. That humbles me."

Her laugh—throaty and enticing—forced him to look at her. He was powerless to do anything other than gaze deeply into her eyes. The ones that shone like brilliant emeralds.

"I want you more than I've ever wanted any man, but I don't know how to be like you. I've spent years alone. I've..." She licked her lips, his gaze following the temptation of damp pink flesh. "...cultivated it, I guess."

His eyes narrowed. "Does that mean..."

She giggled at his stumbling query. "I've had sex before, you know. But it was a release without any kind of emotional tie, which isn't what either of us is expecting, is it?"

"No, Erin. What's between us is a lot more than that. A whole heap more." He willed her to read between the lines, and her smile, tremulous and patently unsure, reinforced that they were looking for the same thing.

She gulped her drink. "And on that note, I should call it a night, before I do or say anything that would be unwise."

"I'll walk you out."

She shook her head, a veil of red wisps. "No. I need some time to think. I'll see you tomorrow." She gazed at him, time seeming to stop...

Should I kiss her? The thought flared bright for an instant. He'd do better to let her go this time. Next time, he'd steal a kiss when she was prepared.

She turned, leaving him at the table and gazing into the red wine. With a sigh, he lifted the glass to his lips and swallowed.

He should call it a night too.

E rin embraced the chill of the night air. Clearing her head was high on the priority list, given she'd just agreed to *something* with David. If only she knew exactly what that *relationship-status-stuff* actually was.

Nerves shattered the calm that had descended once outside. "What the hell was I thinking?" She stopped and looked up, the dark sky offering no answer. She shrugged. "I don't know anything about families, or relationships."

She kicked a small stone with her foot, wondering if she should just march straight back in there and tell him she'd made a mistake.

The very thought of that sliced through her. Sharp and indescribably painful.

A tear trickled down her cheek and she dashed it away. "I've never been some shy and retiring woman, so why now?"

Erin made herself move, head back to her accommodation unit, watching as the winking out of lights reinforced the fact that she was alone.

"Concentrate on the case," she mumbled and rubbed at one temple. "Celeste says she doesn't know Eliana. Liv knows Eliana's signature though. Why? Who's not telling me everything?"

A seed of doubt sprouted in her mind, but she pushed it away. They'd already determined that Liv was telling the truth. *Hadn't they?*

At the bottom on the steps she started up them. First one, then the next level until she moved to the side, on the landing of the third floor, before she was startled to hear rustling behind her. She turned.

Too slow.

It took place in an instant, the blow to her head hard. Sharp, stealing her senses, and even as the black billowed across her mind, she knew she was falling.

CHAPTER NINE

*I*nstinct had David moving quickly. He'd downed the wine then left the bar almost as soon as Erin had left, the need to check and ensure she had made it home beyond any normal kind of sense. It urged him forward, and as he turned at the corner of her block, he imagined her heading up the stairs. Indeed, the sound of muted footsteps made him smile.

He scanned the first flight, and the second.

A sound caught his attention, and as he stepped forward, his heart stopped.

A body lay on the ground near the base of the steps and he moved closer, and in that instant he knew it was Erin.

She lay crumpled and broken on the concrete.

David dashed forward. *"Erin!"*

Don't let her be dead. Please! The refrain started on autoloop, he panted and crouched, fingers curled as if he were afraid of the answer to the unspoken entreaties.

With trembling fingers, he pressed two fingers against her throat and almost threw up, feeling the beat of her heart.

Unsteady fingers dove into his pocket, tugged out the communicator. "Michael? I need you. Erin's been attacked in the accommodation block."

Doors that had been closed opened, men and women gathering, some carrying the 'just woken from a doze' look, while others tugged jackets and dressing gowns around them in readiness for action.

"It's a medical issue. Under control, but did anyone see or hear anything?"

The few that answered verbally gave a negative answer, and he sighed. *What had she seen that meant she was attacked or was she followed?*

He contacted Sevres and Fairburn, Jonah and Daniella.

The first two he requested on site, the other two would be waiting at the infirmary when she arrived.

The sound of running steps echoed loudly, then the few who'd gathered around him parted and Michael appeared. "Let me look at her. The ambulance is on its way, and we'll move her to the medical center as soon as we can." Michael hunched down beside David and put his hand on his brother's shoulder. "Hang in there, David."

Michael worked, checking her pulse, pupils, and neck with a small medi-scanner. Once satisfied, he sought assistance and moved her onto a comforter someone spread out and they straightened her.

"Looks like a blow to the head and lots of bruising, some quite deep," Michael announced.

Sevres muttered something, and Michael nodded. "Yes, I agree. I want to check and make sure there are no fractures or bleeding. The ambulance—"

"Arrived as I did, sir, and they're on their way up," growled Fairburn.

David heard the clatter of the medi-bed on the roadside. It wasn't much, but at least they could start getting her prepped and moved to the medical facility.

With Michael on hand, medical assistance and transportation, he could focus on who caused this. David rose up. "I'll be there as soon as I can. Sevres and—"

"I want to know who caused this," Sevres threw out.

"We all do. One more moment." He turned to Michael. "As soon as

I can I'll be there unless..." He couldn't finish the words, the fear that the injury was more substantial too much for him to consider. Not now that he'd finally got her agreement to consider a relationship.

"It doesn't look life threatening. I'll let you know when she regains consciousness," his brother added.

David's gut churned, but he followed his men some distance from where the medics were transferring Erin to the stretcher.

"She's got a hard head, David. Michael will see her on the road to recovery," Fairburn added.

David fought the impulse to turn back—to check just one more time. He embraced the anger and settled on finding the person responsible.

"Did you see anything odd, David?" Fairburn spoke with a rasp, as if he too were laboring under an intense emotion.

"No. But I heard footsteps, so I was following them, thinking it was Erin. I found her, but the sound kept going along there." He pointed to the walkway.

"Then we follow that thought pattern. We go up. See what we can find."

The three men followed the steps, the third floor empty as the fourth. The team split up with David and Sevres returning to the third floor before meeting Fairburn at the end. "Anything?"

The man shook his head. They made their way down the stairs, glancing left and right for anything. "Whatever they hit her with, there would have been blood. Maybe not a lot but..."

"Yeah," David bit out, unwilling to hear the words out loud. He turned the corner and saw the trashcan at the base of the steps. "Check the gardens around here, Fairburn. Sevres, I want to check this."

He lifted the bin lid then stared. The tablet device lay broken, case cracked and dribbling fluid. "What the..."

"That's pretty damned odd, right there." Sevres spoke softly, peering over his shadow. "Damned straight it is. Do you have evidence bags on hand?"

The man grinned, teeth bared. "I always do." He reached into his pocket and drew out a large, clear sack, used it to lift the item out, then slid it in. "We'll take this back to our lab. We can run the tests there for fingerprints, but it looks to me like an older HMV-551 used by schools. Obsolete tech."

His stomach pitched at that. They only had a few of them on hand. The one he knew to be employed were used by... "*Liv*! Dammit, get someone over to Daniella and Jonah now. Then we need to track the girl down. She's got carte blanche in the base, and she's likely using it to..." He whirled and bellowed over his shoulder, "I need to get to the medical center. Erin, Michael, and Clarissa, plus our lab, could all be compromised!"

His legs pumped as he ran, anger and terror warring deep within him.

CHAPTER TEN

*W*aking hurt. Erin felt the intrusion of something in her hand. Right now it was more than she could manage to swat it away, because the radiating discomfort of her head overshadowed all the other aches and pains.

"Sleeping Beauty awakes."

Above her, Michael grinned though the dark circles around his eyes had her wincing as she attempted to push up. He pushed back, a more forceful act that left her even more achy and dizzy.

"What happened?" she asked.

He smiled. "I thought you'd be able to tell me that. But to keep it short and medically related, you took a blow to the back of the head. Fell down some steps too. Concussion but no fracture or long-term damage, you'll be pleased to know. You're going to have some killer bruising though."

Pleased wasn't quite the way she'd describe it. "Who found me?"

"David followed you. Wanted to make sure you got home safely. Seems old-fashioned courtesy still has its place. He found you, called me and his team. He's now wearing a hole in the linoleum of the hallway."

She moved restlessly as he spoke.

"Don't suppose you'd care to see him? Put him out of his, and our, misery?"

"Oh. Yeah, I'll see him." She did want to see him. Suddenly there was no one else she needed there more.

Michael retreated and returned with David trailing behind. He looked rough, hair standing on end, a gaunt raggedness that had her itching to smooth away his worry.

"Erin! Oh God!" He lunged, hand curling around hers, and she soaked up the sensations of touch and wellbeing that flooded her body.

"David, I don't know what happened, but I have a theory..." Her words slid away as he brushed her lips with his.

"We can talk about that in a moment. I just need to tell you, I've never been more terrified in my life than finding you lying there beside the steps. I wasn't sure if you were alive and, in that moment, everything crystalized for me. Erin, I can't live without you. I don't want to, because you're the oxygen I breathe. Woman, if you ever get yourself knocked out like that again—"

"Wow, now that's a lovely way to talk to the woman you love, isn't it?" A woman's voice intruded from the doorway.

Erin glanced over David's shoulder, seeing Daniella had snuck into the room and taken up position by the door, Jonah at her side.

Erin wanted to blush, or at the least fall through the floor, but she glanced back to David who hovered beside her.

The word Daniella had used... The big 'L' one was clear on his face. She blinked and gulped. *No! He's just worried.* Except, the knot in her belly whispered, what if that's not so?

"Go away, Daniella, Michael, and Jonah. I want to talk to my girl *privately*."

Daniella laughed at David, though it was a sort of sisterly snort, then all three headed back through the swinging doors.

David shook his head. "They're right, of course. Definitely not the way to tell you I love you."

Can a person swallow their tongue? Erin flailed at the stark announcement of love. They'd barely kissed and he just promised her an emotion which terrified her, simply because she couldn't understand it.

"Uhh, Erin?" he prodded.

She closed the mouth that hung open and blinked. "I... I'm kind of at a loss how to respond, David. I mean, I think I love you, but what if I'm wrong? I don't..." Her fingers tugged from his grip and twined together while tears burned because she knew she was fucking-this-five-way-to-Friday. "I..."

His grabbed her fingers once more and squeezed. "I know. It's a lot and you're unsure and I'm a mess. Blurting it out like that wasn't exactly fair to you, was it?"

She bit down hard on her lip until a sting and coppery tang broke through the tangle in her mind. Her fingers clutched at him. "I... David, I don't know what I want, other than to be with you. Nothing else makes sense. I going to need time."

"Then I'll take that, Erin. And we'll see what more there is as we go along." She made to nod then groaned as pain blossomed behind her eyes.

"I should leave you, let you sleep." The grip on her hands told her he didn't really want to leave.

"Unless you want me to stay?"

"I... Would you like me to?"

"I... Yes, I think I would."

"Just let me get rid of them, then I'll be back." Before he left, David dragged the chair closer to the bed, looked from her to the door. "I'll be quick."

"Go," she whispered.

Leaving the room was difficult, but outside, waiting just beyond, was a wall of worried people. "Okay, Michael. Concussion. Anything else?"

"No. I think we'll keep her overnight for observation, but we'll release her in the morning."

David didn't realize he'd been holding his breath, but he released it with a whoosh.

"Good. That's good. I'm staying though. At least for now."

Jonah scratched the back of his hand. "I think that's wise, and given the circumstances, it wouldn't hurt to make it overnight. Fairburn and Sevres reported the situation to me. Daniella..." Jonah turned to his wife, the senator, and winced, "We know who was responsible."

"And?"

"Honey, it was Liv."

Daniella blanched, reached for the chair behind her, and sank down. "No. It... There's no way. She wouldn't—"

David shook his head. "It was her tablet device used to cosh Erin. She's the only one with access to them, who can give us false information regarding Sorrington, after she claimed to overhear us. We know some of the children are trained techs, and I'll bet she's one of them. She has unfettered access to the base, knows the locations of Jonah's office and the lab. It fits." He waited for her to respond to his assessment.

Now his sister shook her head, golden hair flying. "You can't be sure. I mean, anyone could have had the tablet." Daniella was reaching, they all knew it, in the way she clutched at her tunic top, scrunching it up, along with the beseeching look in her eyes. "*Jonah?*"

"It looks bad, Daniella. She's the only one with access to that tablet, as David said. They're all individually coded to their user, so no one else would be able to do anything with it. It's not exactly an item someone would steal, being old tech. She's got free rein of the base when she's not here in the medical center which was a mistake on our part. We trusted her quickly. Possibly too quickly as it turns out, and everyone here knows of your attachment to the girl." At that Jonah simply swiped his hand through his hair, glanced at the agents flanking him. "Our attachment," he amended. "Has she been located yet?"

Sevres shook his head. "No. I'm trying to contact Senna to step in. Assist with locating the girl. While she's free and somewhere..." The dark-skinned man didn't need to finish the statement. They all knew that while the girl was somewhere on the base, she could be up to anything. Sabotaging or collecting intelligence to pass along.

Jonah embraced his wife, who now cried silently into his shoulder. "I'll have the base placed onto alert. We'll double the guards, and I'll send men out looking for her, while enacting a curfew. If necessary, we'll start a building by building inspection."

The strain on the man was clear in the harshness of the planes of his face, but David couldn't bring himself to care about the youngster. He'd almost lost Erin.

"Is there anywhere in particular she may be hiding, Daniella?"

Daniella shook her head. "Not unless she's with—"

"The other children." Horror spread, tendrils reaching through David's nervous system. "You stay with Erin and keep an eye out here. I'll lead the team." Jonah pushed away from the wall. "We need to find her, and if that is where she is, the problem could be bigger and harder than anyone imagines." Then he led the team at a run from the waiting area.

"David, do you really believe that she's to blame for the problems?" Daniella's voice broke on the final word.

He wanted to tell Daniella he was wrong in his reading of the situation. That his team had the wrong way of it, but he couldn't. He refused to lie about this, not just because there was too much at stake, but also because his sister meant too much to treat her with the lack of respect. So instead he shrugged. "I wish I could, Daniella. I really do. But she attacked Erin, she's given us false information and made up a story about Draven Sorrington having a family member called Eliana. We don't know how much damage she's done to the investigation during this time, whether she's accessed the lab where we're working. If she has, then chances are she's also tipped them off to us having Celeste on site, to the line of investigation we're running. It would explain how they gained access to the feeds in our system. What it also brings into consideration, is what she may have planted in the lab. We'll need a full sweep again."

Exhaustion pulled at him, and he rubbed his hands over tired, aching eyes.

"There's too many facets to keep track of. And all of them lead only to death, Daniella. Yours, theirs or hers."

Tears dribbled down Daniella's face, and he crushed her into a hug. "I wish it were different, I really do."

She sniffled. "I know, it's just that I hoped it was wrong."

"I know. I'm sorry, Daniella."

"So am I." When Daniella rose, it was slowly, as if she'd aged decades through the conversation.

"You should get back to Erin. She needs you. I'll go check on Celeste then head home."

He narrowed his eyes. "Not alone. Make sure you have a guard and have them stay until Jonah gets back."

"I'll be fine—"

"No. She's already attacked Erin. You're a target too. Look, I'll arrange—"

"Erin needs you."

He hugged his sister again, a tight heartfelt embrace. "I'll get someone over here now. I don't want you alone at this point."

He moved away, made the request, and it was mere moments when her guard, people he knew, arrived to escort her back to her rooms. Slowly, her returned to Erin to find her asleep, pale but alive. They'd made it through tonight, but until the girl was captured, no one on the base was safe.

Being on enforced rest again chafed at Erin. She wasn't the kind that would easily sit and twiddle her thumbs, but David had become most insistent.

They did, however, allow her to sit with Celeste and gain as much insight as possible.

"So, Lilly Montaine did what?"

Celeste mumbled about the woman's fall from grace that caused a scandal, and Erin made notes, hoping that something in this would be useful. "Of course, I wasn't there at the time," the blonde woman said.

"But that was when Draven came out of the closet, so to speak. He's not worried who he sleeps with, and the more the merrier according to him."

"His relationship though with you is..."

"Oh, not as close as it used to be, I'm afraid. We... I hoped my time on the yacht would kind of soothe those waters. But it didn't. Look, I'm tired now, can we do this later?"

Erin rose. "Sure." Actually, given how much her head ached right now, she was pleased to leave.

The conversation with Celeste going around in circles as she discussed the people she'd associated with, Lilly Montaine and her academic credentials then fall from grace as the darling of the ivy league college she attended and subsequent return home.

Stories of Draven Sorrington and his predilection for breaking rules filled the pages of notes, along with details of social outings and alliances. It was all just foreign to Erin though, and while she noted the facts, they didn't rate high on her rank of importance.

In need of some useful way to spend her time, Erin tracked down to the laboratory. Maylin had come in with bug sweepers and detected three different kinds of devices. They'd been stashed in the computer units and also on their internal comm systems plus in the air extractors.

"She listened to everything we said and did then?" Erin asked once Maylin left and David escorted her back to her room in the infirmary.

David nodded. "She was thorough. Knew exactly what she was doing. Maylin also ran a new diagnostic program she's been working on. The woman found Liv had recoded some of the blocks we'd put in place. Maylin reckons she's probably got more coding skill than any of us thought, given the way it's been crafted. Took her four hours to break the sequencing."

David took another bite of the meal he'd brought to share with her as she swallowed another spoonful of the chowder. She couldn't explain why, but the taste seemed so much blander than when she'd had it before. When he placed his plate on the tray hanging over her bed, she gave up the pretense of eating.

"So, did you get Senna onto the case?"

"Yeah, she was involved in some surveillance so we could replace her easily on that mission. She said the girl hasn't been seen near the building with the children, but that she can't be sure that doesn't mean she hasn't found a way to communicate with them."

Erin closed her eyes, considering the information David had shared. "She's alone. She has to eat. The stores haven't seen her, so either she has a stash or has found a way to access food. The cottage? Has anyone thought to look there? I know it's not quite finished, but certainly it would be somewhere to begin. The weather is also changing, but she only has lighter clothing still. We don't know what she might have in terms of apparel, so we should assume she's managed to access a uniform. That would allow her to blend in." She bit her lip. "I suppose the work on finding the backer has come to a halt?"

He grinned, the color of his eyes lightening, and crinkles appeared at the corner of his eyes. "Not at all. Maylin has the computers back up and running. We should be back in the lab tomorrow, and with Celeste's information, we know that Eliana is a partial ruse, one which Liv exploited. We'll start work on tracking down Sorrington and his financial resources in the morning."

"They're going to release me in the morning." She let the bald statement hang in the air, and he smiled.

"I'm pleased. But why don't you stay with me when you are."

She sat up in the chair, mouth open to argue.

"Humor me, by listening. We've got a problem with the kid on the loose. No one knows how or when she'll strike again, only that she will. Being solo makes all of us targets, so for everyone's sanity, but especially mine, I'd prefer you remained with me."

Erin considered his request, the earnest way he asked. Carefully weighed up the possibilities that went with staying with him. Including the potential intimacy issues. "You're right. It would be better for everyone that we aren't alone. I could stay with Senna, and I guess you could stay here with Michael and Clarissa."

A seed of devilry had planted itself, and his frown was the payoff. David opened his mouth, and she couldn't control the laugh.

"But I won't," she said. "The only thing is, I'm not sure either of us are ready for more. I mean, I'm not sure I am anyway."

He raised both hands, a gesture of not defeat, but acceptance. "If that's what you want, I'll control my baser urges." The grin that flashed died away quickly enough though from his face. "At this point, I'm just pleased you won't be alone, Erin. You're too important to me."

It was going to take a while for her to be comfortable with his frequent protestations she thought. "Michael says so long as I'm sensible I can return to work the day after tomorrow. I'm to be sensible, barring unusual circumstances. He did say I have to be careful not to jar my head." She grimaced. "You know, I never used to be this prone to accidents and injuries. Getting shot was bad enough, but all the stuff that's happened since? It just sucks!"

His bark of laughter made her grin. She'd never thought of herself as funny before, but hey, if that's what it took to make him smile, to see the sexy glint in his eyes, she'd do just about anything. *And doesn't that make me a sap?*

"Want me to stay the night again?" He mock-leered, twitching his brows, but the question stilled the mirth that had risen up.

"I...uh, probably don't need you—"

He reached out, framed her cheek with a firm hand. "I didn't ask if you felt you that you needed me. I asked if you *wanted* me to stay."

She wanted to say yes on one hand, but didn't want to admit that it wasn't about feeling safe. The truth was, she just wanted him close by so they could continue forging this 'deeper connection' he'd mentioned more than once.

"That's settled then." He pushed the tray table away from her bed, then settled deeper into the chair beside her, hooking the other across from it with his feet and resting them on the padding. The blanket he'd used the night before was draped over the chair, but he didn't pull it over himself yet.

"It can't be comfortable," she wondered aloud.

"The chair? Oh, it's all right. After years of stakeouts and sleeping at desks, it's okay. At least I'm semi-flat!"

She smiled, understanding his words and acknowledging the truth.

She climbed from the bed, met his quirked brow with "bathroom" and fled.

Once she'd attended to her ablutions, she waited a moment or two longer. Needing a second to marshal her thoughts and reactions.

It felt alien, having someone waiting for her.

Good, but very odd.

Heaving a sigh, mentally cursing herself as an emotional weakling, she let herself into the room. David had drifted off while she'd loitered, and she took the opportunity to study the man who'd become so damned important to her.

Rings circled his eyes, something she hadn't really noticed before, while the lines around his mouth appeared deeper, as if etched in marble. He was a good-looking man, not muscular but wiry, with a firm packing of muscles though he hid them beneath carefully tailored suits and now his dress uniform.

Even the Kevlar suit had molded to his body in a sexy way.

She liked the fact he was taller, but only by a few inches, so she didn't feel overshadowed by him.

Erin brushed a strand of hair that hung into his eyes away, then on a sigh, she turned, surprised when he grabbed her hand. She turned back to find his gaze sleepy and relaxed.

"Don't I get a good night kiss?"

Her stomach lurched. The power of his kisses was overwhelming, yet the heady promise was far too enticing to ignore.

She reached down, cupped his chin, and brushed her lips along his. The brief flare of electricity wasn't enough; her body her body demanded. But any more and she might do something unacceptable— well, at least in a hospital—so Erin backed away. "Good night."

She retreated to the bed, listened to the cadence of his breathing as it settled, but sleep was a long time coming.

CHAPTER ELEVEN

$\mathcal{D}$avid scrawled the findings on the whiteboard. Visual cues would enable him to consider what had so far come to light and assist in examining connections and planning the next steps.

"Too many threads," he muttered, drawing yet another line and adding notes. "Liv came to us via the hospital. Was she a plant that they hoped would give us false information? To keep tabs on our understanding of the situation," he said, examining the notes he'd scrawled. "She promises to give us information, leads us to the spot in Eastcliffe where we find a nest. Helps us find Olante who gives us the nursery."

"I don't think that was what they planned. Look at how unprepared they were. They didn't expect us to crack him so fast or so easily." Erin pointed to the linkage. "It just doesn't make sense to lead us to their most important facilities."

"But they found us quickly. At the site," he countered.

"True, but I think that was more because she tipped them off, rather than dropping too many details for us to find them. Of greater concern is that we accepted her word so readily. What gave her the believability factor that we accepted everything she said without determining her honesty? Was it arrogance on our part? A lack of understanding of the enemy we faced?"

"Okay, so we were too quick to release her. We've learned our lesson there." David moved to the carafe and poured another coffee, the third so far this morning. It seemed like something was going to happen, and he hated not knowing what or where.

"Sorrington clearly knew we were heading down to talk to Celeste. He had her on the yacht, and when she made contact, she said there was more information. Has she spoken to you about that yet?" Erin waited, tension crackling in the air.

David closed his eyes, considering her question. "I planned to see Michael this morning about talking to her. You said you kept it light?"

"He wouldn't let me interrogate her, so I just focused on making sure she knew she was safe and healing and gathering social intel, I believe it's called."

David laughed at the disgust coloring her tone.

"I didn't think antagonizing Michael was wise," Erin added.

David nodded. "Then we need to see her this morning. Find out exactly what she does know about the plot and see if that clarifies anything."

"At the same time, even though we know there is no Eliana, I think we should continue investigating to see if there are accounts in this name also. It would certainly allow them to channel funds, and yet, although the last name is the same, PolSearch wouldn't detect it as the privacy regulations—"

"Because they don't allow us to connect them together as it's a breach of their privacy."

"David, this could be the break we're looking for. We need something, and the populace is growing restless. The children have gone to ground in the last week, and I've got a feeling something big is brewing. Something we're all going to find hard to cope with."

"I agree. So, let's not waste any more time. We'll head over and catch up with Celeste then—"

David was surprised when she stopped him with a soft hand on his shoulder.

"Uh, why is she called B for Buffy on your phone?"

He started laughing, couldn't help himself because the memory was so strong. "When we were younger, Celeste and I used to watch a heap of ancient vids. There was this one about a girl who attended some kind of day academy. Now, you have to remember, I barely knew Celeste— she was a friend of Daniella's. I mean, she'd come over, but more often than not, I was busy doing something else."

Erin sat still, as if she wanted him to hurry up.

"Anyway, this girl on the vid Daniella used to watch, fought ancient creatures without messing up her clothes or her long hair getting in the way. One day Celeste was over. It must have been summer break. So she decided she wanted to pretend to be this Buffy girl. We were in the garden playing it up when one of the gardeners surprised us. Celeste turned around and kicked him, hard enough to wind him, but she hurt herself more. When the physician came to see her, he made a comment about her actions certainly not gaining her an A on any test and maybe barely a B. Since that day—and I'd forgotten about it, to be honest— I kept her in my contact list on the comm as 'B for Buffy.'"

When Erin simply stared at him, he shrugged. "I guess it was funny at the time." He blushed, heat flooding his face.

She gave a nod, her face grave, then made for the door.

"Erin?"

"Yeah?"

"You've got nothing to worry about with Celeste. We were child-hood acquaintances, and I haven't seen her in years." He needed her to understand that she was the one that mattered to him. Every other woman who'd come before was a pale comparison.

She whirled, eyes twinkling. "You think I'm jealous? I was trying to remember if I'd seen that vid you were talking about... I love ancient vids!"

He stared at her, uncertain about her words. "Uh, okay."

She moved through the door and he followed, totally at sea with the mood changes of women.

He'd not really bothered much with forming deep relationships during his study years, aware that in order to finish his courses, he'd need every ounce of concentration. Over the years, he'd guarded many of the men and women the greater populace lusted after. The shallowness of their lifestyles, and the interests of others represented a huge turnoff. It wasn't a case of he hadn't dated women at all. He had. Just he'd wanted someone in the game for the long-term. Those kinds of women were hard to find.

Outside Celeste's room, he stopped. "Erin?"

She turned, a question in her eyes. "What? Time's kind of short right now."

He frowned, once more confused at her reaction, the way she could so easily put aside her personal dilemmas. "Can I see her first, alone? It's been a long time since we've..."

Erin's gaze roamed his face. "Sure. Go for it."

Taking her words at face value, he slipped inside the room, surprised to note that flowers covered every available bit of bench space.

After David beckoned her in, Erin strode into the room.

Celeste was settled against pillows, her blonde hair fluffed out, smile wide. "So, you're the woman who captured this man, huh? He's a great guy. I've known him since we were both big enough to watch those action vids together with Daniella." Celeste gurgled with laughter, throaty and uninhibited, and Erin simply stared at the woman.

She wasn't here to discuss David, though he bloomed crimson with embarrassment at Celeste's words. Erin had been surprised when he'd requested a moment to see Celeste but had thought maybe he'd been telling her to answer the questions without any personal commentary.

Being left to wait outside cooling her heels had been a surprise, but he'd swiftly opened the door and ushered her inside.

She flicked on the small notation unit. "You're acquainted with

Draven Sorrington, right? In the copter you said you had no knowledge of an Eliana."

The woman in the bed frowned. "That's not quite what I said. I said I don't think *there is* an Eliana."

Celeste's words confused Erin. "I don't get what you mean."

"Draven went to school with my cousins, so I knew him well enough, not that he moved in the same circle as our family. He had this thing, like an alter ego, he'd assume whenever he was up to no good, and he was regularly doing that. But he was indulged as an only child. His parents couldn't have any more, and they doted on him. A lot." The dry tone in Celeste's words made the back of Erin's nape itch.

Erin looked around, spied a chair, then tugged it close and settled in. This was clearly going to be involved. "Okay, so he was indulged, didn't move in the same circles, but what has that got to do with Eliana?"

The woman shot her a look that said she clearly had missed out on something in her younger years. "He would get into trouble. When he was younger it was little stuff. He'd write a note and blame Eliana, or steal the maid's bag because he wanted something in it. Not bad, just uncaring of another person's rights. Seems he thought it was okay, because people would pay him attention, including his parents. As he got older things escalated. One time he stole a car and smashed it because he was drunk. Got involved in some rough behavior. Things like that. When the water got hot, he'd dress up like a woman and call himself Eliana. It became a joke... We'd say 'is Eliana coming to visit today?'"

Erin didn't understand people who acted like that. He clearly refused to take responsibility for his actions. "If you knew he was like that, why did you go out on the boat—"

"Yacht," interjected Celeste.

"Okay, so you went with him on the yacht knowing he has tendencies that are..."

David cleared his throat. "It's a small world in terms of people you can be yourself with. Closed. Friendships are closely guarded in that social strata."

Erin snorted. "Okay, so your small friendship group knew about his tendencies to assume this other persona and use it to behave badly. In some instances, break the law. With all that in mind, why did you go out with him on the yacht?"

"He said he had other acquaintances of ours, that Lilly Montaine and Haran Sintha were going to be joining us."

Erin glanced at David, noting how his gaze narrowed. "You never liked Lilly," he said slowly.

"No. But Haran is engaged to James Framworth. I like him and Haran. So, I was pleased to hear they were going. It was arranged a week ago...or so. Anyway, they weren't on board, and Draven was pulling out before I could come up with a reason to renege."

Erin wrote furiously, inputting the information she was gaining while trying to understand the world where yachts and who attended events were more important than anything else.

"You launched the dinghy and sent a message to David that evening. What occurred to make you feel you were in danger?"

Celeste bit her lip. "Look, clearly you aren't keen on me. I live a life-style of idleness and can afford to get away when the average person has to deal with the day-to-day ramifications of whatever the hell is going on. I get that. I wanted to be a doctor, but my parents vetoed it. Said I needed to do something to fulfill the heritage bestowed on me by my name. So, I ran events, lots of them. Raised money for orphanages and those who live in poverty. One I'd worked with was the Everthorne Foundation."

Erin cocked her head to the side. "I've heard of that one. They fund operations for children who are underprivileged. Rehome orphans—" In her mind, the truth connected. "Oh my God! They're using the Everthorne Foundation?" She glanced at David, who'd bolted upright in his seat.

"I don't know who or what you're talking about, but Draven told me that I'd participated in funding the children who killed. That he needed me to do more, or that I'd outlived my usefulness. It scared me! He looked so cold and disconnected. Then Lilly piped up and said they'd been years in the planning and she would be at the top of the tree finally."

Tears shone in the blonde's eyes, and Erin believed her. But even more than that, came the understanding that the tendrils really did infiltrate every aspect of society. With Jeremy Colvert as a surgeon specializing in reconstruction and initially at the cutting edge of cybernetic therapies and IVF. Ellis Corvino as previous headmaster of Eastcliffe's school, and Olante in the military, the tendrils stretched into the wider community. If they could find the financial backers who were feeding the political arm, they'd have a chance of cutting out the poison. If they couldn't, then the consequences would be far-reaching.

She rose, needing to talk to David privately and sure the rest of the team needed the information she'd gleaned, David following suit.

"Thank you for your time, Celeste. I'd like to keep you on the base for the moment, to ensure your safety. We will be posting guards on your room, and anyone coming and going through here will be scrutinized. Is there anyone we need to contact for you?" David's voice washed over Erin.

Celeste smiled at David. "Just my housekeeper. She'll contact my parents and let them know. We aren't particularly close, so they won't be looking for me anytime soon."

Erin nodded. "I'll attend to that then."

Leaving the room, she moved at a rapid clip, well aware of the man striding beside her. Letting herself into the lab, she noted the startled expressions of Sevres and Fairburn.

"This got a whole heap deeper." Erin found the pen that would write on the whiteboard and ran over the facts they'd got from Celeste. At the end of her monologue silence filled the room.

David stared at the whiteboard, chin in hand. "Keep going, Erin, while I think."

"We need to find a list of the board of directors for Everthorne, those involved in the financial aspects of the same. See what cross overs exist between our current persons of interest and Everthorne.

We also need to follow up with the whereabouts of Sorrington and Montaine."

David nodded. "Sevres and Fairburn, you need to track down Sorrington and Montaine. Bring them in before they have time to go under. Maylin, I need all the financial data on Sorrington, Montaine, and Everthorne. I also want to know if any of them were involved with the school in Eastcliffe and if any were also known to be in contact with Olante and Colvert."

Erin snagged a drink of water, grateful to wet her throat.

"McNally and I will start hunting through the records of the children. See if any were adopted through the Everthorne Foundation, or received any surgeries. We'll also start tracking down the last known locations for carers and children. We've got to find them quickly and bring in as many as we can."

Erin took advantage of the break in David's planning. "Have we found Liv yet?" When Sevres shook his head, she scowled. "Dammit. We need to find her. She's dangerous, loose on the base here. Keep looking."

"I need Michael, Clarissa, and the medicals to list the procedures any children in our custody have been through. We can then try to feed into the medical world this information, given a high proportion of them are against what's happened," David added.

Once more, Erin considered the information on the board. "This is going to get worse before it gets better. I'd like Senna to go under-cover, see if she can sniff out anything we've missed from within the community. She might also be able to tip us off if an attack is imminent."

"I agree," David replied.

CHAPTER TWELVE

*T*he attack came that night. Swift and brutal.

Children, heavily armed, advancing in lines with death and destruction their key criteria. Hundreds of them creating a living barrier around the base.

Small in stature, though powerful and infinitely focused killing machines.

David woke with a start as the alarms blared and pulled them unceremoniously from slumber. The buzzing, blaring jarred as did the strident wail of personal communicators, having received an emergency call to action.

He bolted upright. One glance at the screen told him all he needed to know. He launched up. "Erin! We're under attack!" He hoped the call was loud enough that she'd hear him from the next room.

Climbing into pants, thrusting feet into boots and grabbing the first shirt he could find with speed while the light from his bedside lamp was hardly enough to illuminate the room.

He searched for his sidearm, grabbed it, and shoved through the door, met by the set face of the woman on the other side. "I received the same." She'd dressed and was tugging her hair back into a ponytail. "Grab me my side arm and we'll get moving. They need me at the gate."

Something akin to panic arced, but he fought it down. She was a skilled fighter and they'd need everyone they could get in on the action.

"I'm there too."

"Good. Then we stick together if we can. Let's go."

He followed her out of the tiny apartment and down the stairs. Two of a billowing sea of humanity, ready to go to battle against an army without emotion.

His mind whirred into life, and he snatched up his communicator, connecting with Jonah. "What?"

"Where's Daniella?"

"I sent her to the medical unit. She'll be best protected there." Jonah's terse explanation removed one of the many fears that lanced through David.

He grunted, pleased the man who'd married his sister had made provision for her. "What about the babies?" They'd finally finished the process of adoption, but if the children were coming for them—

"Who?" Jonah bellowed, and David heard a commotion over the line. It was growing difficult to hear as voices called in the masses surrounding him.

"Jonah? Get the babies to the infirmary. Guard them well. I have a feeling they're going to make a play for them. We damaged them significantly when we got them, we have to..."

"Right, I'll send a team over to round them up. In fact, you'd be best since you finalized the placements and have the details..."

"I—" David's mind blanked for an instant. That would mean Erin would go to the front line without him.

Head over heart, and how could he honestly protect one more than the other? His gut churned. The children were innocents, unable able to protect themselves. The battered organ in his chest squeezed tighter, producing an almost physical pain.

David shook his head. *I've got my orders.* "Fine. I'll be on my way in five and will check in once they're all secured." His turn was slow, scanning around, but Erin was gone. His head thudded a wild tattoo. On a growl, he sent a message via her communicator.

Sent to round up and defend babies. Don't take chances. D.

Then he whirled and loped toward the first cottage, knowing full well where every one of his charges had been dispatched to.

For the first time, knowing that Liv was loose somewhere on the base, the fury that continued to grow was dampened by worry and concern. The babies likely only being cared for by one person. The risk to them was great indeed. If Liv was coordinating with those attacking somehow or sending intel, who knew exactly how many others would attempt to infiltrate the base and carry off the children?

I can't allow that. His legs pumped faster.

At the first cottage he rapped on the door smartly. A woman in her early thirties opened the door, the babe cradled in her arms. Before she spoke, he raised a hand. "The base is under attack, and in order to guarantee your safety and that of the babe, I'm here to escort you to the medical facility. I'm going next door to raise the family there. Grab only your essentials and follow me."

He waited as she scooped up the small bag of items he gathered she must have had to hand, a coat and shawl, and followed him down the path to the house next door.

Once he'd gathered the first half dozen, which took far more time than he'd hoped, he ushered the women forward.

The infirmary loomed just beyond them, the echoes and screams, thuds and flashes of light had woken more than babies who wailed as the women scurried, fear making their movements jerky.

David turned, surprised by a flash of movement just to his side. A glance confirmed Liv had jumped out into the roadway, aiming at him, her hair flying and on her face a mask of intense hatred. Features tight and teeth bared, she'd raised her arm, bar in hand.

"They're ours. Give them to me!" Her scream, guttural and wild, told him everything he needed to know. She'd played a long and deep game and had always planned to attempt to regain control.

The girl swung her arm in an arc and the bar flashed in the lamplight.

David pushed a woman in the way to the side, her scream lost to him as the fight-or-flight chemicals urged him to move quickly. He didn't even keep track of the baby she carried.

He couldn't. The danger was too extreme right now.

A whoosh of air sailed past him, followed by the metal weapon.

David groped, the butt of his sidearm in his grip and he dragged it out in a quick motion. Finger to the trigger, he watched her moves, saw them telegraphed as she spun another wide arc.

He lifted.

Fired.

The *pfzt* sound echoed loudly in his hearing.

The girl's eyes widened with surprise. He'd got her center mass, and she arched, arms flying up, fingers releasing the bar that clanged on the asphalt.

She hit the ground with a thud.

It felt like the altercation had taken hours, yet only a moment or two had passed.

Now he stilled, frozen by the ferocity of the attack and the intent in the girl.

"Stay together and get in the building," he ordered the women.

They hurried to obey, and he waited until they pushed through the swinging doors then glanced back at the body before him.

He advanced warily, not sure if the girl was dead or alive.

The scent of charred flesh flared, and his gut churned. He crouched down, touched her throat, and sighed, realizing she was gone. "Dammit!"

David drew his device from his pocket, touched his finger to the call button on his communicator, and connected with Jonah. "I've got Liv. She's dead. We're outside the medical center where she attacked. Her intention was to steal the babies."

The sigh rippled down the lines. "I'll apprise Daniella later. Get Michael and his team to retrieve the body. You've rounded up everyone with the babies?"

David scrubbed at his brow. "I'd got to a dozen. I'll wait until the body is retrieved then go get the rest."

"Fine. Stay in touch." The connection died away, and he tagged Michael, briefly outlined the situation, and waited as a party of three joined him.

"We'll take care of her now. Go get the rest of them."

David didn't wait to see them lift the girl and carry her inside, he only glanced in the direction of the gates, allowed a moment of fear for Erin to intrude, then continued about his mission.

E rin slumped to the ground, exhausted by the break in the fierce fighting. Bodies lay strewn on the ground, the fencing little more than a mangled pile of metal. Dimly she made out the sounds of shouts, cries, and moans that filled the air.

Her eyes ached, her body felt battered, and her mind had yet to switch back out of combat mode.

In the middle of it all, she'd looked for David, but he'd been nowhere to be seen. Then his text had come through, and the terror that gnawed at her abated somewhat.

That had been hours ago. Her sidearm pulsed still, overheating from use.

"Help me," someone behind her cried out, and Erin rose, unsteady, to turn.

Her mind turned slowly, missing the size of the person who called until it was almost too late.

They aimed a fist in her direction, and she dodged, stumbled, but regained her footing in time to lunge forward and grab the teenager who'd tried to jump her.

What the fuck? She'd damn well had enough of everyone trying to jump her, to attack. She grabbed the girl, coiled her fingers in the masses of hair, and tugged. The girl howled.

"What the fuck do you want with me?"

"Not telling," the girl groused, and Erin sighed before twisting the hair. The girl screeched, fingers reaching to claw.

"Look, I've had an absolute gut-full. Tell me who you are and why you're here."

Tears dribbled down the teen's face, and as much as Erin wanted to give up and in, she knew the girl wouldn't hesitate to hurt her. The girl scrabbled at Erin's hand, nails biting deep. Erin cursed loudly and wrenched the girl in her direction, ensuring she pasted her angriest and most dangerous visage on her face. "You tell me, or I'll do far more than pull your fucking hair!"

The girl quivered in her grip. "I don't... They'll kill me."

"And I'll do worse if you don't spill your guts right now." To emphasize the point she lifted the sidearm and pointed it at the girl's head. Her gaze narrowed on the barrel then searched her face.

The fear and stench of bodily fluids told Erin the girl knew she'd use the weapon in hand as the color drained from her face.

"You're Erin McNally and you keep getting in the way of our plans. My mission was to take you, specifically, out."

"What?" She almost released the girl in shock, but shook her head, clearing away the hazy thoughts.

"You're a problem for us. There's a number of high-impact targets and you're at the top right now." The sullenness of the girl almost made Erin smile. Maybe she would have, if she wasn't so completely pissed off right now.

"You lot are seriously in need of strategic assistance if you think I'm that important."

When the girl sneered, Erin twisted the hair tighter, and the girl howled. "We got intel, says you're right in the middle of trying to track down the people at the top of the tree. Can't have that."

Erin knew full well that she'd need to hand the girl over to the security forces on the base. A quick glance over Erin's shoulder showed that members of the forces had already regrouped. Others military personal already worked to reinforce the fencing and provide medical care to those alive after the brief and intense skirmish.

She lifted her communicator and tagged David, who answered. "Erin, you're okay?"

"Yeah, but I have a present for you. Meet me at the front gate with a security squad. I got one walking and talking here."

"What?"

The loud outburst didn't faze her after what she'd seen and participated in. "I'll explain when you get there."

Redoubling her grip on the girl, Erin shoved her sidearm into the soft flesh between the girl's shoulder blades. They moved at a rapid clip to the area by the front gate, only two minutes before David arrived, two guards following him on foot.

The worry on his face eased when he caught sight of her though she didn't acknowledge the force of her own ragged emotions. Here wasn't the time or the place.

"She said she was sent here specifically to neutralize me. I caught her as she was sneaking up, we engaged in hand-to-hand. As you can see, she's been overpowered." Erin noted the way David's mouth thinned at her declaration, but there was only room for the truth, and heaven knew, she'd had enough of the rubbish from these young killers.

Shoving the young woman into the guard's arms felt good. Righteous even.

"We'll want to interrogate her later. Put her into solitary for now. Check for hidden devices." David's voice rasped, and Erin frowned, realizing for the first time that his demeanor wasn't just concerned; there was more there.

Something had occurred.

Something bad.

Her hand fisted, aware that she couldn't ask him right here and right now what had happened.

Keeping still, holding some distance between them until they'd marched the girl away took every ounce of willpower. Once out of sight, Erin grabbed his wrist and pulled him into a dark area behind the guard's post. "What happened?"

For all the fury on his face, David shook his head. "Later." The single word was all he uttered as he slipped from the dark, her gaze taking in the carnage before them both.

"They came for the babies, didn't they?" she asked.

Now his eyes took on a distant look. "Something like that. They're all safe though."

Jonah came striding through the mess, his face grim. "They were prepared to throw these ones away in order to gain control of the babies. I wish I knew why." He scrubbed his hand over his gaunt features. "I need you two back in the lab, following up on your leads." Jonah turned, then slid back in front of David. "You handled a difficult situation well. The women told me about Liv's attack and your swift action. How it saved them and the children."

Erin's heart lurched. No wonder he didn't want to discuss it. She reached out, instinct overriding everything else, and placed her hand on his in a gesture of understanding and solidarity.

David flinched but waited for Jonah to leave. "I was going to tell you later. Away from here."

Erin dragged her hand back. He hadn't pulled away, but neither had he seemed to want what she was offering.

It hurt. A tiny piercing of her heart.

He felt alone, that she understood, but the need to be there for him, to ease his pain, as scary as it was, grew. The need was a living entity in its own right.

He led the way, slowly picking their way through the mess, toward the center of the base. There were others who'd clean the place up, reinforce the fencing. This wasn't where they'd be best used now.

Erin didn't look back.

CHAPTER THIRTEEN

*A*nger and frustration formed an uncomfortable alliance in David's mind. The anger he felt at the loss of so many lives, without a reason, was something he just couldn't understand. Whoever was still pulling the children's strings clearly saw them as disposable.

The loss of Liv in particular rode him hard.

He knew he'd done what was needed, having seen in those seconds that she felt no empathy, that her emotions that she'd used to gain freedom had been nothing more than a sham. Guilt took up a corner of his mind too, as he realized he'd accepted her actions and words at face-value.

Topping it off was the knowledge that Daniella would be devastated.

In the middle of the maelstrom was the panic he'd felt not knowing Erin's location. Or even if she were still alive. It had only been after he'd seen her that his heart once more resumed its usual rhythm.

He'd never been so pleased to see her. She may have been grimy, face blackened and exhausted, but she'd never appeared more beautiful to him.

"Erin…"

She stilled, turned her gaze on his, her eyes soft as if she already knew what he struggled with. Her light steps brought her beside him. She started to raise her hand then stilled, gaze roaming over his face.

"I killed her. Liv. She was going to take the children. I had to protect them."

Understanding flared in her eyes. "I'm sorry, David. She attacked first?"

Unable to speak past the lump in his throat, he nodded.

Erin cupped his cheek tenderly. "You had to protect them. She did what she had to, ensuring that the children would be returned. You did what you had to, making sure they'd have a chance at a family and a future. I know, because I understand you. You'll tell yourself there must have been another way. Something that would have got through to her. I doubt there was ever any hope of that. You need to forgive yourself or the guilt will eat you up."

The kiss she brushed over his lips was soft and healing. David closed his eyes, reached out and shook as she gripped onto his shoulders, pulling him closer.

Passion flared, bright and overwhelming. Snapping his eyes open, he speared his hands into her hair and dragged her close, needing the power of her kiss to banish the ice that seemed to settle around his heart.

Lips tangled and breathing became something he had no control over as the roar of hunger filled his brain.

She met him, his every move countered by hers, urging the passion to boil over, scalding them both with its heat.

When Erin tugged away, panting and red-faced, lips swollen and bee-stung, he couldn't think beyond the fact that she was the most amazingly beautiful woman he'd ever seen. "Erin, I…"

She slid her finger across his lips. "Work first, then pleasure." The humor in her words punctured the bubble he seemed to be encased in and he sighed.

"You're right. Later."

Her smile was soft. "Definitely. Later."

The kiss in the lab doorway had scorched; Erin's mind and neurons were probably fried.

She chuckled at the thought before sobering. It didn't change the fact that David had been hurt by having to deal with Liv. She could understand that. It wasn't just the girl had drawn them all in, but the fact she'd attacked him. Not for the first time, Erin wondered if the duplicity in Liv's actions hadn't broken a part of David's soul.

Fairbairn and Sevres entered the room, Maylin in tow, and the trio settled in with the new information they'd gleaned from Celeste.

"I've found the last bug. A clever little creation inside the communication systems. I think it's how she managed to communicate with the others and we didn't even know." Maylin's rueful comments stopped everyone in their tracks. "She was an even better coder than we thought."

Sevres muttered something, and Maylin scowled.

"I also found listings for Eliana Sorrington. Financial holdings, stocks, property, and even currency. She or he built an impressive portfolio. Not enough to bankroll the entire thing, but we're getting closer to the truth." Maylin grinned across the room, and Erin noted that although there was an air of triumph the team was also drooping.

A quick glance at the clock told her they'd passed the three AM mark. "We should pack it up and come back fresh in the morning."

"Don't you mean later this morning?" Sevres ended the question with a yawn, and she looked away, unwilling to share in the exhaustion the rest of the team carried about them.

"Something like that. We'll meet back here at oh-nine-hundred hours. I'm going to set some further runs for the comps to run remotely. When we get back in, we should have more information."

She rose, as did the team, and waited as they filed out.

On silent feet she moved to David, who'd remained at the comp, fingers clicking at the keyboard. "Coming?" she asked.

Without a word, he rose, took her proffered hand, and followed her to the door.

CHAPTER FOURTEEN

*I*t was a moment in time David was sure would remain in his memory. Erin's fingers curled around his, excitement zinging wildly in his system and a heady sense of intoxication brought on by her proximity to him.

They didn't speak, and he was sure it was as if they were communing mentally, both agreeing to what was yet to come.

At his room, he stopped her, tugging Erin into his arms so that she felt the same body-to- body contact, wordlessly asking one last time.

Her smile assured him, and he dipped his head, kissing her lips, the conflagration sizzling just below the surface.

He tempered it, knowing full well that to indulge now might have them on the floor of the stairwell.

Erin mewled as he spun away, sliding the lock-card over the fastener on the door. It snicked open and he drew her inside.

"Erin?"

"David." Her breathy words filled him up, fanned the flames.

I'm going to take this slowly. He wanted to savor every last minute of what was to come.

Knew this would be his last first time, and surprise skittered at the rightness of the emotion.

He stepped forward. "I want this to be right."

She laughed, an almost inaudible sigh. "So long as it's with you, it will be." Never taking her eyes off him, she reached for the buckle of her belt and tugged, let the tongue slide out, then it sagged. "So, where should I..."

He gulped, the sound silenced before it could echo. "Uh, on the seat." He indicated the small tub chair in the corner of the room, hoping she wouldn't see the shake in his hand.

Erin grinned as if reading his discomposure and moved, more like a sashay, to place the gunbelt down on the seat.

David shook his head, feeling more like a high school boy with his first serious girlfriend than an adult. His body was hungry, the need clamoring. He urged it to still. Instead of giving in and grabbing her, he turned, unfastened his belt, and hung it in the small cupboard.

His arms shook as he fisted his hands, trying to grab control of his senses. At this rate, it would be over before he started.

David didn't hear her but jumped as she wound her arms around his chest. "Wanna start a fire?" she whispered.

He trembled as her breath teased his skin and set nerves to dancing.

He turned into the embrace, amazed that after false starts and missteps, Erin was finally here with him.

Sliding his arms around her, feeling the way she crowded close, he exhaled, slowing his heart rate. "You're so beautiful, Erin." He bowed his head and captured her lips, the suppleness and warmth giving way to the warm, wet cavern of her mouth.

Their tongues danced, twining as the heat surrounding them grew in intensity. His hands roamed, finding the dips and hollows of her body. Molding the soft curves of her breasts. Yet soon, that wasn't enough. He craved the touch of silken skin he knew hid below the ugly uniform she wore.

He tugged away, feeling slow and slumberous, catching the glint of hunger reflected in her gaze.

"Let me get you a little more comfortable." He reached out, fingers flicking button after button until her shirt gaped wide, revealing pale skin to his ravenous gaze.

Erin laughed, and he watched her flat stomach move with the throaty sounds. "So, I'm all undone, but you're all buttoned up."

The double entendre had him quirking a brow. "Really?"

"Let's do something about it, Lover Boy." Her fingers found the top button and toyed with it before sliding it through the hole while her tongue tip slid to the corner of his lips, and he groaned.

Erin moved to the second button, her fingers grazing his chest, and he flinched as the arc of electricity seared him.

"Let me." With a gentle move, he pushed her hand aside and quickly divested himself of the shirt. Erin followed suit, and he looked his fill, her small breasts hidden beneath a plain white bra.

It could have been the world's most expensive lingerie or an old, ragged item of clothing for all he cared. Right now he just needed her naked.

David's hot gaze was eating her up, and that was a major turn on for Erin. Her body was smoking with the intensity, so much so that controlling the quivering of her arms and legs, let alone her belly, was something she was sure she'd have to give up soon.

Seeing his bronzed chest in the dim lighting stole her breath. "David?"

He reached for her, hands at the snap and zipper, freeing her body, before pushing the pants down her legs, so all that remained was the puddle at her ankles, where they caught on her boots, and her underwear.

Her body bore the scars of her job, and for an instant, the need to hide them rose. But she beat the instinctive movement back. He knew about them, how they'd come about.

"We should..." He pulled her close, and she stumbled. They both looked down, heads colliding, and she pulled away, rubbing at her forehead. David sighed. "Dammit."

He sounded so aggrieved that she laughed. "Oh, David, let's just get ourselves naked."

Under normal circumstances he was sophisticated and assured. Only with her did she capture sight of the uncertainty. It made his reaction more intimate to her. As if he didn't want anyone to see below the surface to the real David.

Her heart mushed further at the thought.

He grunted, and Erin couldn't contain the smile as she set to the task of divesting herself of the clothing. The knowledge that he was just as affected settled her nerves so that by the time she was nude, it wasn't so hard to stand before him, bare in every way possible.

"You're so beautiful." He reached out for her, and she stepped into his embrace, the shock of skin-to-skin making her moan.

Tendrils of pleasure snaked through her body, the peaks of her breasts sensitive dots of hunger that grazed his skin. Her knees wobbled as the searing flare of need filled her belly, melting her in all the right places.

When their lips met, they clung then moved to devouring in a split-second, while they surrendered to the hunger neither could ignore.

David gripped her, fingers digging into the flesh of her butt, lifting her so she could feel the jutting, hard length of his erection.

She gasped and lifted her legs to circle his hips, and impaled herself, the shocking intrusion filling the empty spaces within her body, mirroring the way he'd filled her heart.

He grunted in her ear. "The bed."

"Who needs a bed?" Then she moved her legs, dragging him deeper within as her heart raced madly.

His lips found the line of her neck and she arched, trembling and holding onto sanity as the pulsing began deep within. She sucked in a breath as his moves turned savage, the slap of flesh joining with the musky scent of arousal.

"Erin..." Her name became a chant, the rasp of whiskers stroking her flesh as the screaming orgasm, whirls of pleasure that spiked and vibrated, drew her into a web of passion that seemed to exist forever.

Strong fingers dug deep into the flesh of her waist, and the sound of his groan dragged her back from the place she'd existed. She panted furiously, desperate for oxygen to fill her lungs, her body spent. Erin felt more like a quivering mass of jelly than a woman who'd just participated in the most savage yet tender loving of her life.

Opening her eyes took willpower, but was worth the effort to see David as exhausted and relaxed as she. "Well..."

There didn't seem to be words to explain what had occurred.

"Wow. That was... You're amazing." His voice was hoarse, and she laughed, suddenly feeling lighter than ever before.

"I think we were amazing." She disentangled herself and almost fell, her legs still shaky. "But we should find the bed before we both fall down."

He looked as shell-shocked as her, so between them, fingers entwined, they tottered to the bed.

A thought surprised her, and she muttered, "Should we be, you know, this comfortable?"

David tugged her close. There wasn't much room in the small, narrow bed, so spooning or her lying over him—and didn't she grin at that thought—was the only way they'd both fit into the bed.

"Maybe, or it could be that we've both wanted and needed for so long that we'll just skip that uncomfortable step altogether."

They lay there quietly, then he spoke again, the rumble of his chest vibrating against her back. "Thank you, Erin."

Tears of emotion burned against her eyelids. "No, David. Thank you. Without you I'd still be alone."

Morning came far too quickly, but David took a moment to savor the feel of Erin in his arms. The morning after was as amazing as he'd hoped for. Yet, for all they'd declared themselves to each other, danger still lay around them. The future was dark and uncertain.

Erin wiggled in her sleep, and his mind returned to her. To the future he could hope for.

The truth was, marriage was what he wanted, but whether she was ready, he didn't have a clue. Them as a couple was new. Untested.

They also had to find out who was behind the financial backing of this damned war. The people had started to grow weary, the warrior children carefully trained not to take action against the average man.

"Someone behind them has the knowledge of how to handle the public, right?"

David started at Erin's groggy query. "What was that?" It was true, every step they'd taken had been more of a PR disaster.

"One of the things that seems to happen is we come out looking like some kind of aggressive army, beating up on children, unable to protect our base. For all that we're getting Daniella's regular updates out, they're only targeting those who could be considered..."

"Wealthy and privileged."

She half sat up, colliding with him so her silken skin brushed his chest, and he hissed as the hunger flared just as hot and bright as last night.

Unable to stop himself, he reached out, only intending to tug her against him at the waist, but his hand cupped her breast, and she arched with a small moan, little more than a whisper.

His body fired again, and he sighed, leaning down to place tiny, dotting kisses along her shoulder.

She wriggled closer, turning so he could see the pleasure sheen her skin a delicate pink and her eyes turn into deep pools of need.

He muttered and swooped, their lips once more locked as she mashed her breasts against his chest, darts of pleasure that abraded his skin gently. The kiss was scorching but brief, feeding the hungry passion that filled him up.

David twisted, tugging her so she lay supine against the bed and he loomed. "I need you again."

"Ditto," she whispered.

This time he meant to pleasure her, not just give into the hunger that roared and snapped like a living beast.

He did just that, kissing the fine line of her jaw as she clung, then moving down the length of her neck and into the curve of her shoulder.

She writhed beneath him, murmuring incoherent words of need. When his lips found the furled peak of one nipple she arched, fingers digging into his shoulders, bringing flashes of pleasure-pain so he groaned against her skin.

Erin quivered. "Don't stop, David."

The entreaty urged him on so that he had to savor the other nipple before working his way down her flat belly, only stopping to softly kiss the large scar at her side, saying a quick, thankful prayer that she'd survived.

He slid his hands between her legs, parting them so he could find the tiny pleasure nub before settling his mouth on it, delighting in her musky taste, the way her clitoral hood hardened against the tip of his tongue, his fingers whispering over her moist, wet center.

She thrashed. "David!"

The keening sound, the dewy moisture coating her skin, and the rapid pulse fanned the flames of desire.

Erin scrabbled, found his arms and tugged. "I need you in me, David! Please."

His own heart hammered a tattoo that couldn't be ignited, his body hard and his cock ramrod straight with desire.

He pushed up, setting his lips against hers, and found the cradle of her thighs. "This is what I need. You. Always you. Day and night for as long as we are."

He slid partway, panting and battling for control over the senses that scattered. She moved, and he gripped her waist. "Wait."

His demand echoed, and she opened her eyes, which were hazed with passion. "David?"

He puffed and panted, dragging her close. "Marry me, Erin. Make this what we have forever." Now unable to hold himself in check, he thrust deep, feeling the wet pleasure of the slide, the heat of her body. "Marry me, Erin."

"Oh God! Oh God! Please. Yes!" she screamed, and her orgasm

exploded, body pumping and gripping as he released himself deep inside her.

Over breakfast David expounded upon what he thought about the public relations disaster this brutal war was turning out to be.

"So, they've been picking off only those who could be considered to be the wealthy, and those who have a stake in the old ways."

Erin took a bite of a peach and considered his words. "So, the attack on Celeste, the placement of guards in various locations—"

"Leaving alone places like the settlement where Astrid and Jude are, is likely part of their drive to get enough people on side so that they will accept the changes. That level of thinking is straight from the top in my opinion. Look at the argument they put up before Yin was killed. That it's about protecting everyone, but especially those who can't protect themselves."

Erin nodded, carefully considering the nuances David mentioned. "So, the army is merely an extension of the old status-quo and needs to be removed. What about the children though?"

He sighed and scrubbed his hands across his eyes. "That part is only because it's someone else. So many families lost people in the war that they don't want to lose more members. That's the only explanation I can come up with."

"Okay, so you ran some background searches last night. What do you think..."

"I was looking into who'd been attacked so we can cross-reference the data with what we find in Sorrington's financials. Plus, I was looking into the others who were on board the boat with Celeste. I think they too have connections to the financial backer."

Erin placed the peach pit on the plate and wiped her hands, suddenly nauseated by what was suggested. "They lured Celeste onto the boat, prepared to kill her if she didn't accede to their demands?"

"That's how it reads to me." He took a long pull on the coffee. "And that's worrying, because we don't know who else they've pulled into the web."

"What if it's another Liv kind of situation?" she asked. When David frowned, she reached over and grabbed his hand. "We've been there once, David. What if she's also stringing us along? I mean, I don't like the idea that we're being duped again."

He glanced away, and Erin wondered if she'd overstepped the mark.

His lips thinned. "We don't. All we know is that Celeste is our best lead at this point, and if we don't follow that up..." Then he shrugged. "We should get over to the lab." He rose, but Erin remained where she was. "Erin?"

"I need to shower and change. Go ahead, and I'll be there soon."

Horrible thoughts, the kind that could undo the fragile connection between them, rose in her mind. She couldn't banish them, because not being sure brought everything into question.

She needed to talk to Jonah privately, share her reservations. David wasn't doing anything wrong, but what if he were wearing blinders? They'd already been there and done that, and David seemed disinclined to consider that Celeste was another red herring put in place to blind them.

He waited for a moment then gave a curt nod. "Okay, I'll see you in the lab when you get there."

Her stomach churned as he walked away. Once he'd left the mess hall, she beeped Jonah with her private communicator. "Jonah? It's McNally. I need to talk to you privately. Can you get away?"

"What?" The surprise in his voice met with the pounding in her skull, the tempo a steady and painful cadence.

"I'm in the mess, but I need to talk to you. I'm wondering about some facts, and you're the best to raise them with. Can you meet me?"

The silence stretched, then he agreed and named the armory in ten minutes. Erin hurried from the building, and taking great care, she hotfooted it to the small, squat building, thankful it was closer to the large building she was currently accommodated in.

Jonah had already arrived, and Erin didn't waste any time. "Jonah,

I'm concerned. After Liv," she said, noting that the big man winced, "we now have Celeste. She's given us some information, but it feels all too easy. Like we're being pushed down a path with only one outcome. David feels that the public relations side is where they're beating us hands down, even though in hand-to-hand combat we run rings around them. They're picking targets that will increase their satisfaction rating among the lowest social-economic areas. The fact that Celeste just popped up, leaves me wondering if this wasn't just a little too convenient. I tried to raise it with David, but he's known her all his life, even if only distantly, and seems to be struggling with any question that we're being set up."

Jonah frowned and considered her words. "So, what do you want me to do?"

The words she was about to speak were rocks in her chest, heavy and with the ability to drown her. "I need you to authorize me to investigate Celeste more closely, without it impinging on David's line of question, which I think does have merit. I'm just worried he's—"

"Wearing blinders?" He scratched his head, looked upward, then sighed. "Fine. I'll authorize it and warn Daniella. Just keep a light touch. If he catches on..."

Misery at what could happen was enough to have Erin nodding. "I agree. Thanks."

She felt Jonah watching her as she scurried from the building, well aware time had passed and she'd best hurry before David started questioning where she was and why she'd taken so long.

The shower was cold, however, the clothing was clean. She shoved the dirty clothes into the box at the bottom of the wardrobe, reminding herself she really needed to take some time and do her laundry. Then that was forgotten as she tugged on clothing and her boots and left the room at a run.

S omething was up with Erin. She'd been like a cat on a hot roof all day. Her workload continued to the same standard, yet she seemed disconnected from the rest of the team.

David's mind said to cut her a break, given what had passed the night before, but it didn't feel like that was the whole answer to what she was wrestling with.

"Erin, have you got any results yet for Lilly Montaine?"

She jumped. "What? Oh yes, only daughter of Senator Montaine and his late wife Vandra. Thirty-four and unmarried. Achieved a low-grade degree from Xevia College in Arts Collective Organisation and was employed until recently by Marylou Gantry at the World Bank. That came to an end about four months ago."

He wandered over to her console, wondering why she turned her notepad over, then dismissed it as over-sensitivity.

"What was her role?"

"Social Convener and Diarist."

He slid his hand over her shoulder, wondering with a frown why she tensed before releasing the muscles. *Does she regret—* David cut the thought off before it came to a conclusion. This was work time, and he'd concentrate on that if it was the very last thing he did.

"I need a full financial breakdown on her and Marylou Gantry."

Erin nodded and turned back to the screen. Again, he pondered her odd behavior, then gave up, guessing she was uncomfortable with the looks the rest of the team had shot their way all morning.

At lunch, when David came to invite her to join him, she shook her head. "I promised to catch up with Senna. She's got—"

Frustrated, a thought occurred. "Ask her to join us then."

Erin gave him an 'are you kidding me' stare. "Uh, girl talk stuff, David. Can I take a raincheck?"

Now he knew something hinky was going on, she'd never claimed 'girl talk' before. "Erin, are you—"

"Look, David. Senna and I have an arrangement, long-standing and important, and I can't just blow her off. Besides, I think it's best if during the day we go on as usual, so there's no talk."

It felt like a dismissal. Hell, he *knew* that it was, and he fumed. "Fine. I'll see you back here when?"

"Give me a couple of hours. This one is going to be a heavy session."

He raised his brows, and she paled. The urge to reach out and reassure her raised its head. "Sure, everything is okay?"

Tears glinted near the surface of her eyes, and even as he moved to enfold her in his arms, she slid away. "Yes, everything's fine."

She was lying. He knew it. She knew he did too, and there wasn't a darn thing he could say to fix whatever was going on inside her head.

When she slid out of the room and he was left looking at the open door in confusion, he let her go.

She'll tell me when she's ready. If only he could believe that.

E rin pumped her legs, looking for Senna in the old, disused sheltered area at the very edge of the base.

The woman waited in the shadows, her face a mask. "So, what's up? Besides you and David, of course."

Erin sighed. "I'm not going there."

Senna laughed. "Didn't really think you would. So, what's on your mind, McNally?"

"What did Jonah tell you?" They'd been carrying on a covert conversation most of the morning, arranging for Senna to join her on the investigation into Celeste's background, connections, and possible duplicity.

"Not a hell of a lot. He just said he needed someone he could trust to work with you on a high-security investigation."

Guilt rode Erin, but she dragged Senna deeper into the shadows, found an abandoned seat, and sank into it. "David brought Celeste Landry in after we received a mayday. She'd been on a yacht with Sorrington and another woman after being invited to join friends who didn't turn up. He's known Celeste all his life and refuses to accept that maybe she's a plant, just like Liv. When I suggested that he didn't take it so well. Given the situation with Liv, I felt we needed to question her motives. He isn't open to it. I spoke to Jonah, laid it out, and..."

"And David doesn't know, hence the way this mission is being framed."

"Yeah." Misery flooded Erin's words, and Senna looked at her with a quizzical expression.

"It's eating you up. Why not let me take on the investigation, that way you don't have to..."

"No, Senna. See, if she's not who she claims to be—and to be honest, it feels far too convenient at this point to be believable—then I need to be there. This whole situation is a bloody mess. The people are starting to question what we're doing, the children keep attacking and dying. It's a fucking mess, and I'm distrusting of a long-term friend of my lover—" Erin opened her mouth wide, horror at the admission filling her as Senna stared back.

"So finally. After the shit that went down when Daniella was attacked and you were shot, we've all been taking bets on how long it would be before you two finally got it together."

"Shut up, Senna. It's not like that." The waspish tone just made the woman grin more, and Erin felt horrible about the outburst.

"Okay, so where do we start?"

"I need to talk to Haran Sintha, who's a close friend of Celeste. Apparently, she was supposed to be on the yacht. I need some background, somewhere to start. That seems to be the best bet. I've got intel that she's holed up in one of the luxury hotels in town. We could do this by communicator, but I think it's best if we—"

"Go to her. Sounds fair. When?"

"We can go now. I told David we were having a girl talk and it would take a while." Senna laughed, the sound like a braying horse to Erin's mind, and it abraded at her nerves.

"Let's go. We should talk girly stuff on the way so you don't have to lie to him about that."

The trip was quick, a small vehicle for two, covered with extreme armor plating, taking them to the location as it zigged and zagged through the streets. Erin kept watch out the window, taking in the small barrows that ferried goods and building materials. In the short while since the war had been raging, the place already looked ragged and torn to bits.

"What I don't understand is what would any of them have to gain?" Senna said. "I mean, let's look at this logically. Celeste has been Daniella's friend for how long?"

Erin bit her lip. "Most of their life. Daniella and David have also known Sorrington, albeit not well. David didn't think he'd be involved, but we uncovered his dual life. We're also investigating other connections, which have cropped up from what Celeste told us. To be honest, after the situation with Liv, where we believed her because she fed us some stuff, I guess I'm looking to make sure we aren't duped again. David doesn't want to believe Celeste might be not quite honest." The jitters in her stomach danced like crazy. She knew he wanted to believe, and hell, she wanted to believe too, but reason said she had to lock down the truth beyond any shadow of a doubt, hence going around his back to check. It felt wrong on every level, but that was her job.

"Okay, so what do you want to know?"

Erin rubbed her finger over the bridge of her nose. "If Sorrington is living a double life, then why? Is Celeste any further connected to him or Lilly Montaine? What are her affiliations?" Ticking the main points off on her fingers, she realized that if she found out that Celeste was fabricating the story, she might need more corroboration before David believed her. "I need to find someone else too, who could corroborate the story we've been spun."

They arrived at the hotel, security clearing them with lightning speed, and they settled into the salon with Haran, the red of her gown a contrast to her dusky skin tone. "You have questions about Celeste? Why?"

"I'm sorry, ma'am, but I'm unable to disclose the details of the investigation with you. I just need you to answer a few questions."

They proceeded with the interview, which ended some twenty

minutes later, the woman having backed up all of Celeste's claim except that she'd been scheduled onto the yacht.

Leaving the building with her mind whirring, Erin frowned.

"Well, I guess now you need to talk to the senator." Senna's dry words had Erin's throat constricting.

"Yeah, I guess." As she spoke, the communicator blared, and she stared at the screen then swore.

"Uh, hi David." She flicked a glance at Senna's face.

"Where are you?" His tone brooked no prevarication. She bit her lip, wondering who'd ratted her out.

"I'm, uh..." She fished about, wondering what exactly to say.

"I know where you were. You were questioning Haran, who contacted Daniella who contacted me. What the fuck are you doing?"

Hurt and fury shone on his face, and she felt uneasy. "Can we discuss this when I get back to base, David?"

"No, McNally, we can't." The tone of his voice grated at her. "In fact, I don't want you on my team. I should be able to trust you, but you go behind my back. White-anting me, bringing my team and this investigation into question. I told you this morning, Celeste was not involved."

A frisson of fear lodged in her mind. "David, given what had happened we needed to—"

"No, McNally. You should have trusted me on this. That's what *partners* do." The emphasis on the word didn't go astray, and Erin felt it like a blow to the solar plexus.

"David..."

"No, McNally. I've requested you be reassigned. Immediately." He disconnected, and she stared at the communicator, tears welling in her eyes.

"He took that really badly." Senna spoke quietly. "It's not the usual way with him."

Erin couldn't summon up an answer to her comment, the pain far too great right now. "Let's get back to base."

The communicator blared once more, but she ignored it, feeling emotionally battered and bruised.

"Are you going to answer that?" Senna nodded to the small device she'd dropped into the console.

"No."

When Senna's blared, she could barely raise interest, lost in her world of misery until Senna answered a comment with "Fuck!"

The harsh swear word seeping into her mind, Erin whirled. "What?"

"We have to get to the World Bank. The children have gathered and there's hostages. They want a trade. The senator for the staff."

The roads were practically empty, so when Senna turned the car in a screaming one- eighty there were no blaring horns or near collisions.

The engine roared as they tore up the road, taking turns in careering jerks until the building lay ahead.

Erin's communicator blared once more, and she glanced down. Jonah.

"We're in sight of the building, Jonah. What do you want us to do?"

"I'm sending you in, Erin, to negotiate on our behalf. We aren't surrendering the senator. Find out something they will accept. There are twenty-nine staff members still inside. They cut off the tunnel exit after someone tipped them off."

CHAPTER FIFTEEN

*D*avid didn't usually wallow. It wasn't in his nature, but the hurt and breach of trust Erin had shown him knifed him to the core.

He let the emotion bubble and brew in his chest until the call came from Jonah that stopped his heart in its shuddering beat.

"David? I need you on the communicator with Erin. We've received a demand from the children. They're holding hostages at the World Bank. Erin's the only operative in the field currently with the skills to negotiate. I want you shadowing her, feeding information and assisting."

"What?" His fury melted like ice beneath a baking sun as he realized exactly where she was and the danger she faced. "Who's with her?" His voice shook as did his hands. He'd been hurt, frustrated. Right now, though, he'd take back every word and every action if he could be there with her.

"Senna."

He shuddered, then his hands moved, summoning Maylin and her magic fingers.

"I lost it with her."

"I'm aware of that, David. I've just spoken with Daniella. Erin came to me because she felt..." He sighed. "It doesn't really matter right now. She just wanted to protect you and had concerns. I should have told you, but the case she put up was strong. We needed to be sure, given our earlier mistake."

That rattled David. Erin had wanted to protect him, and he'd flung his hurt and disillusionment at her, barbs he knew would hit home in the most painful way imaginable.

He wanted to scream that she'd faced enough demons, but the awareness that he'd added to them had him cringing.

When Maylin arrived, she set about reconnecting the unit he'd commandeered to the world. Time ticked by, every second tearing at him. Finally, Maylin activated the connection and he could see and hear.

Erin was making her way alone up the road. He texted her: *Where is Senna?*

The grainy vision of the feeds from the buildings showed her looking down, pale but resolute. She reached into her pocket and engaged her secure earpiece and his beeped. He slid it in.

"I left her at the vehicle. Someone has to be able to move quickly."

"Erin, I—"

"Not now, sir. I have to concentrate."

The determination on her features, coupled with her words, hacked at his heart, pain constricting the organ in his chest.

Within a block, she stilled, raised a hand. "I've been sent to parlay."

They turned, the sea of children, faces blank, and a young man, perhaps twenty or so, advanced. "We don't negotiate."

Erin held her ground, her expression grim. "No, maybe not. But as we won't be giving up the senator, you're going to have to think again. What do you want?"

Into the earpiece she whispered, "Get Senna into the building and lead them out through the secondary tunnels."

The children moved, like automatons, and he wondered how they were connected, just seconds before he realized their intent.

"Get out of there, Erin. *Run. Run now!*"

Before she could turn, they were on her, earpiece squawking and squelching then cutting off along with the vid feeds.

E rin knew she was in trouble the moment the children turned in her direction. She could have attempted to run, but there didn't seem to be much in the way of reason to do so.

In her mind, the tag *dispensable* was once again tattooed on her forehead. So she waited, until surrounded, the noise fierce as they roared at her.

One brave girl tugged the earpiece from her then ground it beneath her feet. Truly alone,

Erin waited, not giving into the chants from the children. Senna would find the secondary tunnels and lead those holed up to freedom. All she had to do was keep them occupied.

The man loped toward her, the sea of bodies parting to allow him access.

"So, I don't yet know who you are, but you're trusted if the great man Jonah, now husband of the senator, was willing to send you to negotiate." He rifled in his pocket and pulled out a bag of nuts, carefully removed one and inspected it before popping it in his mouth.

Clearly, this was a tactic he thought would—maybe not break her, but reinforce her vulnerability—yet she refused to be cowed. She'd seen the truth with her own eyes. Interrogated more than one of the children.

"So, what's your name?" Erin asked.

She merely watched him as his smile grew wider.

With a flick of his hand, four young girls advanced, metal bracelet restraints were handed over, and he clasped them around Erin's wrist. She didn't fight, knowing that they itched for a reason to use their skills on her. And she had no intention of making herself into a bigger target right now.

"Fine, we'll simply take you into custody. Given you exemplify everything our kind are fighting against, we can make you our display piece." His shrug lacked empathy, and horror chilled her. He was one. Older, trained, but not lacking the violence that bubbled below the surface.

I'll have to tread carefully with him. He's the scariest one I've come across so far.

CHAPTER SIXTEEN

*U*rgent nausea clawed at David when the vid screens failed. "Get it back online!" His roar was met with a soft shake from Maylin.

"I can't. They've cut the feed, and the best I can do is try to find a nearby location with a camera." Her hands flew over the keyboard, her face strained. Time ticked by. "David, there isn't one."

"There has to be!" *God knows, I can't lose her. Not now, and not like this.*

The screaming inside him overrode every bit of training. His woman was in grave danger, prisoner to the child warriors. They could kill her, or worse, turn her into another Clarissa. Memories of Clarissa's implants and the tests they'd run swamped him, and bile rose in his throat, burning and sickly-sweet.

Jonah arrived in the room and listened to the situation report with a grim face. "We'll find her, David. They won't keep her."

"I was cruel to her, Jonah." The words were ragged, as if he'd been screaming for hours. His hands shook, and he could barely look the man in the face. "When I knew what she was doing, I told her I was requesting a transfer for her. That she'd broken my trust. When I tried to—"

"I know, David. You were hurting and lashed out." Jonah patted his shoulder awkwardly, but David threw him off.

"Fuck that, Jonah! I hurt her. Found the deepest way to do it, then twisted the fucking knife!" His eyes burned, and the pressure in his chest resembled a boulder.

Maylin continued working on the system while Sevres and Fairburn started contacting anyone they knew in the general vicinity.

Senna beeped them. "I've got them all out, except Gantry. She refuses to leave. There's a disturbance in the bottom of the building though. I think..." Her words died away, and his gut shifted.

"You think what?"

"That could be another lab. I mean, it makes sense. Central location. Access to funds and—"

His mind worked slowly as if churning through the competing data loads. "Makes sense," was all he could manage.

"We're going to need a team." Jonah pushed David into a chair while he felt the shock settle and rock him. Then he blinked, once then again.

"They're going to know about the secondary tunnels now. We can't access through there. Storming the front door won't be an option either."

Jonah speared him with a look. "No. But what if they've decided to only put a light guard on the main tunnel? They know that we know—"

"And strategy isn't their strongest skill." It was a long shot, but worth checking out.

"Senna, do you know where the main tunnel entrance lies? Is it possible to check it to see—" Jonah demanded.

"Give me a minute. I'll duck in and take a look." Senna's words echoed.

The feed went dead, and he knew it was to make sure no one could use their beacons to triangulate Senna's location. They may have managed to scramble the systems, but it felt like forever.

"Look, at least the scientific and hacker communities aren't working with them. We've managed to lock down most of our communicators now, and the net systems," Maylin offered.

David grunted, fingers curled into white fists as they waited.

When the blare came it had him bolting up in his seat.

"I think we're onto something, but we're going to need Sappers. They've tried to block the entrance, and while I managed to run a scope through, the hole isn't big enough for us to get through. And there's no guard, so I guess they don't expect us to try that as an entrance." Senna spoke quickly as if she were moving at a fast pace.

Maylin tapped David's shoulder. "I don't see any traffic in or out around the area. I've hacked every camera in a seven-block range, and I've found the location of Senna's vehicle but nothing else."

He'd take that and hope they were on the right track.

"Let's get a team together and get moving." He rose and Jonah opened his mouth. "What?"

"I want in."

David considered the request then nodded. "We'll need Michael on standby too."

It hurt to say the words, but they were necessary.

E rin sat in the cold, windowless room, somewhere in the basement of the World Bank. Marylou Gantry had briefly made an appearance, then whisked away, confirming Erin's thoughts. She was in to this up to her neck.

The restraints they'd placed on her were clumsy and crude but extremely efficient. Her wrists were bound in metal and fastened to loops on the metal table welded to the floor.

How much time had passed was hard to quantify, but she surmised no more than an hour. They'd left her alone after the brief visit and she waited, silently focused on the door.

The room was cool, her skin chilling ever so slightly, and her gaze roamed until she found the air-conditioning vent. Large enough for her to get through if the opportunity rose.

The door opened with a squeak, and a young girl entered, followed by the young man she'd spoken with earlier, taking up position on the opposite side of the table before slumping to the seat waiting there.

"So, Erin McNally. We pulled your records before you shut us out of the system, but you know that already, since you have LN-03 as a political prisoner. We are prepared to trade. Her and all the infants you stole in return for your freedom."

He settled back in the seat, steepling his fingers, apparently unconcerned and expecting her to merely accede to his wishes.

She remained silent, neither willing to acknowledge his offer or give him any kind of formal recognition.

This didn't sit well as time moved on and she didn't answer. His lips pursed.

Erin watched and waited.

"Do you plan on answering my request?"

At this time she thought silence was the best answer. He was uncomfortable with that, and he shuffled his feet. Somewhere deep inside her psyche she knew this was dangerous ground to tread. He could kill her, turn her into a human guinea pig, or worse. Her training told her that name, rank, and serial number were the only answers she should give. *I'll be damned if I give them even that.*

"Answer me!" His roar and the way he shot up in the seat told her he had little control over his emotions. Spittle landed on her face and she left it there, dripping, because the outburst reassured her she was on the right path.

Instead, Erin fought the smile that wanted to form, kept her gaze passive, and watched.

He wrenched the seat up, wobbled slightly then stopped, before searching her face and grinning. The movement of his mouth wasn't echoed in his cold, distant eyes.

"Fine then." He carefully placed the chair on the floor and beckoned to the young girl. "We'll let her consider her actions." He turned slowly, shuffling his feet, then left the room, but at the door he turned back, his grin feral. "I hope you like the dark."

The door locked, and the lights went out.

Her reaction was instant; panic welled.

She couldn't see, locked in a room and fastened to the damn table. Erin didn't fear the dark, but this was different. A sensory deprivation of another kind. Fear rose, and she battled it back, hoping like hell this wasn't going to be a long, dark end.

D avid seethed as he waited for the dark to settle so his sight would optimize for the lack of light. His people had stopped several streets away, and they'd trickled in one and two at a time, gathering in the basement of one of the hotels.

Senna passed out the coded earbuds to the team as he scanned the blueprints on the table before him with Jonah at his shoulder. "You're sure this is accurate?"

"They were all I could find. Do you know how hard it is to find blueprints that aren't electronic? Most of these are old and have been digitized and disposed of. With the Tech Crash in '21 most of the older prints were lost. This is the only one still on file, and I had to pay a lot to get someone into the municipal building to find them." Senna bared her teeth, and he checked the location again.

"Okay, so we put Michael here." He tapped a crossroads, two miles distant, far enough away that there would be time to get him out if necessary. Michael might have the super-strength and speed thanks to his cybernetic implants, but he was also their best surgeon as well as David's brother. The government couldn't afford to lose him.

"We need a team about halfway along, to reinforce our people. About here." Jonah stabbed at the paper with his finger, and David agreed. He assumed that they would face great numbers in the bank. They needed to find Erin and Gantry. Once they had the other woman in hand, his team would get her back to the base for interrogation. "Gantry?"

"Necessary to find out what she knows, but Erin is our priority at this time," Jonah offered.

David knew Gantry now was the key to finding the head of the overall operation.

Jonah had explained he'd finally made contact with bases on the rest of the continents, but none of them had substantial information. All they could be sure of was that this group had sprung up, seemingly overnight, and moved en masse to overthrow the government.

David remembered that the files they'd retrieved from Colvert's office had been indicative of the number of possible pregnancies he'd implanted, which totaled thousands. Add that to the numbers in the gestational tanks in one facility alone, and the numbers would be too large to calculate. Of course, Colvert had continued some of his legitimate work, a cover for his research.

They hadn't managed yet to find all the other scientists who'd worked on Clarissa either, so in theory, if there were dozens involved in the implantation and cybernetic therapy together with nano-infusions... If they were all moonlighting...

David pushed aside the thoughts. He couldn't let the negativity swamp him. Too much was at stake. They needed Gantry, and he needed Erin back.

"We move in ten." Jonah had continued speaking while he'd been considering what they knew, and he shook his head, attempting to clear the fog in his brain. "You going to be up to this, David?"

He pierced Jonah with a look, his hand steady as he rolled up the map. "I'm going in. It's my team and my op."

"But you're also emotionally involved. Mess this up and the work of months goes down the drain. We keep this quiet, clean, and we can use it to build a PR campaign. I've got selected team members I'll be gearing up with cameras so we can show exactly what's going on. Get the word out, so people understand what's at stake."

David snarled. "Maybe, but Gantry and my girl are our primary consideration. We get in, get both, and get out."

Jonah released tense muscles, and David realized he'd been goaded to ensure he was capable of the mission. *Fuck that!* Agitation warred with determination. *I'm going to get her back.*

Thrusting the map into the cardboard roll, he threw it to one of the team. "Get that to Michael. Take five men and protect him. If it gets hot, get him out."

He stalked into the center, his people flanking him. They were good personnel. Well- trained and committed to seeing this through.

"We have two targets," David said. "Gantry. She's the older woman we think is involved in running the show. A backer but not the head one. We get her, then go after Sorrington. They know who's the apex. We have one of our own in there too. McNally. Bring her out unharmed and alive." They nodded, and David indicated to Senna. "I want you to head the secondary force. You're key to making sure we get out in one piece."

Her nod was all he needed. Senna would do the job and his path would remain clear unless they were overwhelmed.

"We move in five."

The cold had long past seeped into Erin's bones, chilling her core, and she shivered again, each move abrading the skin of her wrists. "Never thought I'd go out like this." Her whisper barely registered even to her own hearing.

She'd kept her eyes closed, keeping the rising panic at bay seemed easy at first, but as time wore on and she remained in the dark, jitters and fears rose.

Her thoughts turned to David as she tugged at the metal bracelets circling her wrists. They stung, but she refused to allow herself to despair. There were already enough other things to get upset about in her life, and she didn't need to be adding to the mix.

"I should have told him." She sighed again, knowing that wasn't really an option. He'd been unable to look past what he knew of Celeste, and someone had to check the information to ensure it was accurate.

Of course, that was how she'd ended up here in this mess, but she had known, with twenty-three being held hostage—twenty-two if she amended the figure, knowing now that Gantry had been part of the overall plan—there'd been no option. She'd been trained to help people, to save them. That was what she did, and she was good at it.

"Shame you weren't so good at saving yourself." The words came out on a hiccup. The black, greasy clouds of panic set in again, and she focused on breathing. In. Out. In again.

Once again, Erin tugged at her bonds. "Fucking things!" Tears started dribbling down her face, whether because of pain from her wrists, fear that she'd be left in here in the dark forever, or that there'd be no escape, she wasn't sure. "I won't give in."

A click at the door and the flash of lights had her cringing away.

"Ahh yes. Getting to be a bit much, is it? All this darkness?"

She opened her eyes, squinting at him as he nibbled on an apricot-like stone fruit. "We can do something about that," he said. "Just tell me what I want to know."

"No." The sound emerged as a croak.

"*Tsk tsk.* Those wrists look sore. We could release you. Administer first aid." He slouched against the door jamb, hands sliding down the molding, and she'd couldn't miss the oddity of his movements, as if his legs were about to give out beneath him.

Erin refused to accept his offer, even though the temptation was huge.

He waited in silence, and more time passed. With a heavy sigh, he tottered from the room, and once more, the snick of the lock echoed and she was plunged into darkness.

Crouching, David waited as the sappers tugged the rocks from the tunnel. They moved slowly, soundlessly, and he fought to contain the agitation and frustration. If only they'd move faster. But the most senior one had explained that they needed to be sure the foundations hadn't been compromised. That caution also kept their work silent.

David waited, fumed, and glared at the blockage. Three hours had passed since they'd taken Erin. The not knowing ate at him, gnawing at his mind, constantly grating away until all that remained was fear and fury.

At one point, one of the men clearing the way raised an arm, and they waited, still and silent until whatever the threat was passed. He moved back, next to David. "Seems they're running a circuitous path. No one on duty all the time. We're going to have to move faster, but that increases the danger all around."

Putting aside personal concerns, he quickly calculated. "How long have we been here?"

"About an hour, sir."

"Get them moving. Take every care, but we need to be through in the next half hour. I also want to know what their surveillance schedule is."

The man moved away with a nod, beckoned to the others, and they sped the work up, one rock at a time, moving in a chain, until there was a crawl space for David and his men. One man ducked through then returned.

"If we put someone here, with a couple of rocks, he can make it look like no one got through. That might give us a little extra time."

David considered the words and nodded. "They'll need to be able to move quickly when we come back."

The organization took place quickly. Some carefully whispered instructions passed, then he and the rest of the team scrambled through the crawl space and into the bowels of the building.

Silent hand motions indicated the direction he needed them all to move. Careful motions, checking around corners, flattening against the wall while all the time scanning for video devices had them inching forward.

Strangely enough, they didn't find any in this section. He would consider that at a later point, but right now it served their purposes.

He checked on the four men, wired to collect the data and vision for Jonah and Daniella to release.

The basement area was a warren of small rooms and hallways. Once or twice he stilled the team and checked the tiny photo he'd taken of the levels.

"There's several small offices on this floor, and I say we check them first. If they're holding McNally, that's the most likely position. Down one level there are several larger holding rooms. If they've got labs and the like, that's where I'd be placing them."

But where would they find Gantry? Clearly, she didn't have the medical background and had been on record saying children weren't a part of her long-term plan. David took that as a flag that she likely didn't have much to do with the warriors.

They'd need to disable the children too in order to gain access to the upper levels, and his hand moved to the oneirogenic anesthetic he'd packed, together with the extra, small breathing mask he'd shoved into the space really only meant for one.

They would insert the gas canisters into the various points of the air-conditioning system when the time came. For now, he'd settle for finding Erin.

The first small office was empty as was the second, and David frowned, noting that the lights in this section had been dimmed to almost total darkness. Donning his night scope, he hoped like hell this wasn't part of some elaborate trap.

Three more doors led to offices in this space, and he tugged at the first one, surprised to find it locked and no light shining within. With a shrug, he moved on, opening doors two and three while an itch grew at the back of his mind. *Where is she?*

His mind skittered back to the room he hadn't gained access to. No light, true, but sealed tightly. He started to move on, then hesitated, and gave in, backtracking amid the query of, "Where you going, sir?"

At the door once again, he rattled it, frowned, and patted in his pockets until a small secura-device came to hand. It was designed to short-circuit any lock. He stopped and wondered if they'd alarmed these rooms.

He deployed the device, sliding the electrically charged strip against the lock, and listened for the snick.

Pushing the door wide open, he took a step inside, then stilled. Erin was there, slumped on the table.

Anguish constricted the muscle of his heart as he noted the oozing blood at her wrists, which were fastened to the table with metal restraints.

Moving forward, he inspected the injury site, and she roused. "I'm not... Go away."

"It's me, Erin." His hand searched for the fastening, and his stomach crawled when he realized these were antique-style lock and key bracelets. The secura-device wouldn't work.

He beckoned to one of the sappers, and they patted their pockets, then extracted cutters. It only took a moment to release her, then David bent down and tugged her into his arms. Her skin was frigid, and there was an oddly blue tinge to her lips. "Dammit." He couldn't leave, being in charge of the operation, and he turned to Jonah. "Get her to Michael— something's wrong."

Handing her over took every ounce of willpower he had. It felt like he was handing away a piece of himself, but she was in no fit state to join them.

Jonah took the woman in his arms and fixed David with a stare. "Get the bastards." Then he slipped away.

With Erin once again safe, David's secondary mission kicked in. Find and detain Gantry.

CHAPTER SEVENTEEN

*E*rin's skin prickled and she gasped, the cold that had surrounded her seeping away and replacing itself with an acute form of discomfort.

I'm moving. She tried to open her eyes, but the effort was exhausting. The heat that radiated from whatever held her scalded her, and she tried to edge away.

"Stay still, McNally. We're nearly there." She knew that voice well. Jonah.

"What..." She licked at her dry lips, trying to work out what was going on and failing. Erin slumped, waited for her mind to tell her it was once again playing tricks, like it had on hearing David's voice. *He hates me, so why would he come to my rescue?*

Erin dismissed it as part of the hallucinations she was clearly going through and let the darkness surround her again.

*D*avid's team moved through the corridors and found the stairs to the final basement level. Strangely, there were no guards there either.

It didn't make a whole lot of sense. But then understanding flared. The children weren't good at strategy and planning. Perhaps that was why no one was posted down there? *I hope that's all it is.*

The area would have been cavernous, except the holding rooms, four large blocks, filled the zone. Each one had a single access door. Looking at the team, he silently divided them up into groups of eight. "One on each door, the others to go in, subdue as necessary. Deploy masks." He whispered his instructions and waited as they moved.

The team he remained with took the nearest door and fanned out. He tugged the secura- card once more from his pocket, waited for the snick, then wrenched the door open. A single canister of the gas popped and fizzed as it rolled and filled the air. They'd be out in seconds, given the concentration of the gasses. It was a new-from-old technique Michael had come across during his training. Apparently, in the ancient times, tear gas was used to subdue, but this was a sleeping formulation, and the first time in centuries something like this had been deployed. *I hope it works!*

"Sir, room contained." The first officer followed by the second and third checked in, then his team checked and cleared their room.

"Get vision. We need everything you have, then hotfoot it back to our secondary location."

Assertions echoed, and he peered into the room, unsurprised to see more rows of gestational chambers. In this room, at least ten rows of twenty were empty. Another room contained a similar set-up, though there were only a few infants sleeping in the chambers. The third holding now gassed combatants.

The fourth was a barracks like set-up, with bunk beds giving them some idea of the force they'd find in the building. One hundred and thirty-four combatants. His team only numbered twenty-something. The odds were bad, although they'd found forty in the previous room they'd subdued with the use of the sleeping gas.

He sighed. "Leave the rooms as they are for now. While they're all asleep, including the attendants, we're safe."

They reformed at the base of the stairs, all eyes on him, waiting for further instructions. Where would Gantry's office be? Likely at the top of the building, he supposed. But that would mean thirty-six flights above ground and surveillance. And somewhere in the region of eighty children, if this one barracks was the only force employed in the room.

Of course, this couldn't be all of it. They'd need training rooms, a mess hall, and likely at least a medi-center. If he were planning the layout of the building, those would be in a secure location, somewhere near the top. Where the everyday people wouldn't see them. Access would also pose a problem. Unless the security officers knew about the children, there was another accessway, or elevator. Likely without cameras.

"Follow me." He led the force to the main elevator banks and spoke quietly—near a whisper. "There's got to be another elevator point. One that doesn't show up in the building."

Dragging out the photo he took of the building plans, he thumbed through to the eighth floor and peered intently, looking for a space or false wall. At the right-hand side of the building, he noted a space, crossed out. That could be what they were looking for, so he led the team in that direction.

"And here it is." Before him was a black painted door to an elevator. "Get that open so I can have a look." He looked at the call button, aware there'd be an alarm, and pumped the faceplate, smiling as it opened wide. Wires of yellow, blue, green, and purple filled the space.

"Anyone got cutters handy?" He knew they did; after all, they'd just released Erin.

Someone extended a tiny hand-held device, and he searched his memory. Purple was the security color code. Holding his breath, he snipped the wires, then grabbed the small scanner out, connected it, and over-rode the safety feature so all anyone watching would see was a momentary glitch.

With a groan, the doors to the elevator shaft opened, and he peered up. The capsule was on the floor below, and he smiled. "I need to get into it, get up to say level twenty-eight, then make my way from there. Any volunteers to come with me?"

The lead sapper stepped up. "I'll come. Once the floors are secured, we can get the rest of the team up there."

David nodded. "Sounds like the best option we have. We're going to need something to pry open the doors."

"I have just the thing." The man smiled, and David was more than sure he did, given the array of odd items hanging from his utility belt.

Without a sound, David jumped, grabbed the wide metal thread of the elevator pulley, and climbed down. Once there, he lifted the small door open and peered into the cubicle. "Empty. No surveillance." He slid within and moved to the side.

Surprise filled David as he realized there was no security swipe on the doors, but he just shrugged and tapped level twenty-eight. They'd collected a bag of canisters from the rest of the team, theorizing they may need multiple on each floor.

The box lifted slowly, and he watched and waited, the numbers flashing before his eyes. Twenty-five, Twenty-six... At twenty-seven he tugged a canister out, prepared it, and as the door opened, he deployed it, thankful they'd both replaced their masks. Children dropped in the doorway within seconds, and David, along with his sidekick, moved out of the enclosed space.

He knew there was an air-con input on each floor, so that various fresheners and cleaning gasses could be released into the system. He hooked a can to the input, and the two of them headed for the stairs. Once inside they listened, but there wasn't a whisper. They repeated their actions on each floor, careful to avoid detection.

On the thirty-third floor, he stopped the sapper. "We need the others up here."

The man nodded and whispered into the headset, while David checked on the layout of the final floor. Two rooms and a hallway.

"We'll need to move quickly," David whispered, and the man nodded again.

With luck, the majority of the children had been immobilized. They'd already come across large numbers, so he could only hope his guestimate was close.

They waited before the elevator door, considering and planning. "I need five in the lift and the rest with Holscomb," he called softly, indicating to the sapper who'd worked with him.

Picking the men and women he judged to be quick and agile, he moved into the elevator and glanced back at the rest of his team "See you up top."

On the jaunty words, he pressed thirty-four and the doors slid shut.

Erin woke again, warmer but still exhausted, to see Michael peering at her from some kind of ambulatory vehicle. "Where... Where am I?"

"Safe. We're just waiting on the strike force to return. They've already sent back four men with video evidence to release once the team is safely back on base."

She blinked. "What strike force?"

"The one that got you out and is heading up to the floor where Gantry is most likely hiding out. They found another nursery and two gestational units, plus a rather large bunk room. Right now they're clearing the nest."

"How long was I out?" She struggled up into a sitting position, determined not to be either a victim or considered infirm.

"You were taken nearly five hours ago. We've been warming you since Jonah got you here, and he's waiting on the team."

Considering Michael's words, Erin frowned. "Where's David?"

"Leading the team."

"Shit!" Erin ripped the covers off herself and swung her legs to the side of the bed, groaning as she wobbled. "What the fuck is wrong with me?"

Lethargy tugged, and she growled.

"Hypothermia. They were slowly freezing you. Your core temp dropped dangerously low. It's taken forty-five minutes to stabilize your temp, and you're damned lucky you didn't lose any fingers or toes. Get back into that bed. Right now, McNally."

Pride shrouded her. "I don't need it. I need to be in the field, not lying in a bed being all helpless."

Michael laughed at her and pushed her left shoulder.

She slumped and stared at him. "Why did you do that?"

"Because you're in no fit state. However, if you promise to behave, I'll let you sit up front and watch the action when we're apprised."

Erin seethed at his words, but acceded, realizing she wouldn't be any use to anyone in this state. *I'm really over this being useless crap.*

CHAPTER EIGHTEEN

The door slid open soundlessly, and David and the others in the cubicle deployed the gas. On every other level the concentration had kicked in swiftly. This time, with more at stake, David had to hope it wouldn't fail him.

"I hope we didn't overdose them," one of the recruits beside him muttered.

He hoped so too, and they moved into the corridor. "Set off two in each room. Make sure to throw then close the doors and drop. We don't know what weaponry they have."

The team split up, moving to the doors, and at his nod, they followed his instructions.

Tense moments passed. Some gunfire echoed but was quickly stopped as those in the rooms clearly succumbed to the gas.

"Floor cleared." He spoke into the earbud and waited for the recognition by Holscomb. Once acknowledged, the team made their way up the stairs and assembled.

"I need Gantry. There was also an older kid, early twenties. If he's on the premises, I want him as well. There's something about him."

David's team moved like clockwork. Gantry and the young man were located and carried to the elevators. Their exit from the building took place through the small exit at the tunnel. David had no intention of telegraphing that they'd taken the building just yet.

Too much to do and clear. The last thing any of them needed was some kind of remote detonation, if indeed the building was wired.

"Get me a camera and we do each level, every room. Whatever we see, we tape. Any records we find, confiscate. Watch out for surveillance."

They scattered, moving down to the floor below, checking each and every room. Each child was tagged and restrained until they could make plans for dealing with them.

On the thirtieth floor, they found the medical center. A full operative suite and compact command center. File tapes were collected and plunged into deep backpacks so they could be examined back at the base.

Two medics lay supine beside a table. A girl on the table was also asleep with her legs in stirrups. "Shit!"

Judging by the instrument one of them clutched, they'd been preparing to implant an embryo. The other medic held a small sonic device David knew allowed them to undertake ultrasound scans.

He shook his head, released the girl, and carried her from the room, unable to leave her there. Thrusting her into the arms of one of the waiting men, he muttered, "Get her out of here. Just make sure you restrain her first. They were about to implant." David knew he sounded angry, but he couldn't control his reaction to the horror of what he'd seen.

If he had to guess her age, he'd place her around fourteen or fifteen. Far too young to be a human womb donor.

He restrained the male and female medical staff, revulsion filling him. "They should pay for their actions, sir," one of his men said.

Privately, David agreed, but he kept his silence.

On angry feet, he stalked to the lift, pressed the down key, and headed for the tunnel. The sooner he checked on Erin, the better he'd be feeling.

Hefting the backpack over his shoulder, he watched as the sappers removed the last of the rocks, a steady trickle of personnel moving back and forth, transferring those they'd taken prisoner out of the building. It would take time given the numbers they were dealing with, and they'd arranged to annex a local hotel until such time as they could clear those they held and found alternative holding facilities. There simply wasn't room on the base for this many.

The medics he'd directed to have moved to the base, hoping they were the missing clues for the team who'd worked on Clarissa.

Feet and head aching, he spied the vehicle in the distance. The door slid open, and there she was. Still, pale, and fragile, but very much alive.

David checked himself, remembering back to his last words to her, and catching sight of the wariness in her eyes.

"Erin..." He reached out, and she shrank back, just a little, but enough to warn him that he'd need to tread carefully.

"Agent Villede, sir. I've posted a request for a transfer." The huskiness in her voice unmanned him. Her eyes brighter than emeralds with unshed tears of hurt tore him up inside.

Fuck me! "Erin, please. I spoke harshly, and I was wrong."

Her chin moved up, and he knew exactly what she was doing. The tiny physical movement a shield in case he hurt her further. He couldn't let this go on, he told himself and moved closer, crowding her.

"Dammit, Erin, I was wrong. I hurt you. I know I did. In hindsight you were right, and I was blind. They were questions that should have been asked, by me. I didn't, because for some reason, I wanted to believe, even after the thing with Liv, that we couldn't be gulled again. Because we trusted her, and were proved wrong, and we nearly lost the babies, but I didn't see how I could possibly make the same mistake again."

Her smile was wan. "You were right to trust her."

"No, Erin. I should have trusted *you*. You've never lied to me but looked to protect me from myself. I was so damned wrong in the way I spoke to you, the fact that I didn't listen. I know it's going to take a lot for you to trust me again, but baby, if I have to grovel, I'll do it.

Whatever it takes." Burning scratched at his throat, his eyes steamed up, and his voice broke on the last words.

She blinked, lips forming a tiny smile, and the ice which coated his heart melted just a little. He hoped like hell he was reading the situation right and he hadn't messed up the best thing that ever happened to him.

"Okay, so we need to get her back to base, and you've got a date with the interrogation unit, from what I hear. Get in and we'll give you a lift." Michael had snuck up on them and was grinning widely, no doubt digesting the bit about groveling.

David waited for Erin to settle back on the gurney. He strapped her into the bed at Michael's behest and took the seat opposite.

Confusion seemed the best way for Erin to describe the roiling emotions she experienced.

David had apologized and seemed to mean it, but he'd hurt her. His lack of trust and anger diminishing the so-called connection between them.

She wasn't the kind of woman who held onto anger, believing that it would harm her at the most basic level of her psyche, but the distress that speared her couldn't be ignored or wished away with just a few words.

Throughout the drive, David remained silent, studying her with a grim but watchful gaze, almost as if he could read her thoughts.

When they arrived back at the base, before they went their separate ways, he stilled her with tender hands. "Erin, I know it seems unbelievable, but I am sorry, and I need you to forgive me. Think about that and the way we felt together. Don't let this push us apart. Please?"

"I'll..." She hiccupped, started again. "I'll think about it." Then Michael whirled the gurney and pushed it into the infirmary.

She could have looked back, even reassured herself, but she had to protect herself and her heart, the one she'd guarded zealously throughout her long, lonely childhood and into adulthood. The one she'd taken a chance on, only to find that he'd undone her. Come close to destroying her in his anger.

Tears welled. The gurney stopped just inside the doors, and Clarissa moved forward and folded her arms around Erin.

Just like that, Erin couldn't control the tears. "Oh... Oh gods!" Dissolving into a puddle wasn't like her at all, but the pain and fear poured out, just like the tears she couldn't stem.

Clarissa helped her down and into a small room, where she sank into a seat, the tissues Clarissa shoved into her hand sopping up the mess.

At some point Clarissa left Erin alone for a moment or two and returned with a hot drink. "Drink this, it'll help."

Erin dried her tears and accepted the cup, the warmth scorching her still tender skin. "Thank you."

The nod Clarissa gave her together with the troubled gaze left Erin sighing. "I didn't mean to melt on you like that."

"I know. It's all a bit much when things happen like that, isn't it? But you've had a huge shock, your body has been all but frozen and David acted like a fool, all in one day. I think it's okay to lose it."

A bubble of laugh erupted between Erin's lips, and Clarissa grinned at her.

"Men aren't the brightest creatures ever made. They make these mistakes then have to try and undo the damage they wreak." Clarissa sighed. "It's our job to let them work through it. After all, if we make it too easy, they'd never learn. Now, I believe that you're supposed to be resting, but you've spent a lot of time lately in recuperation in medi-centers, so I have an idea. Come upstairs. We've got a spare room, or if you prefer the living area, there's a sofa. We've got vids on tap."

Erin cocked her head at the woman who was David's sister-in-law. It didn't make much sense to her that she'd invited her to head to her private living area. Wasn't she supposed to be on David's side?

Clarissa laughed when she said that to her. "No way. We girls have to stick together, and Daniella said she'll pop in later, once they've got some information to share. I wouldn't be surprised if the guys don't join us too."

I'm not sure how I feel about that. Of course, it wasn't her place to tell Clarissa who she could have in her home, so she remained quiet and allowed herself to be ushered upstairs.

The room was comfortable, with the throw rugs slung over the squishy chairs and a coffee table covered in files reinforcing the feeling of homely chaos.

Clarissa disappeared into the kitchen, taking Erin's mug with her. The ding of the food heater echoed, and when Clarissa returned, it was with a tray adorned with two drinks and a bowl of crunchy nutty treats. Clarissa passed her drink, now warmed through, back to her.

"These seats have rising stools built in, so try them out." Clarissa showed her how to engage the footrest, and when she did, Erin welcomed the sense of well-being.

"Erin, I don't mean to pry, but are you okay with everything that's happened? They held you prisoner in an alien environment, deprived you of lights, and you were fastened to the table, according to Michael. When you were found, your body temp had dropped. That's a lot to deal with."

Biting her lip, Erin considered the soft question from the woman opposite her, understanding this was as much a therapy session as a break from the sanitized rooms below in the health center.

Her contemplation must have taken longer than expected, as Clarissa nudged her with an "Erin?"

"I'm trying to think about what you've said. I guess it will cause me some points of concern later on, but I was doing what I was trained to do. Keep my mouth shut, wait it out."

Clarissa frowned. "And the taken prisoner bit?"

Erin smiled. "No, but my task is to save people, and I was taken while giving Senna time to get them all out. They did all get out, right?"

"Yes, except Gantry, who we realize is working with the warriors. She's been taken for interrogation."

"Ahh."

CHAPTER NINETEEN

"So Marylou, you're a contributor to the warrior children project, being well aware that they are integral to the overthrowing of President Yin and the government. You are also charged with funding the bio-technical development, the nano-technical infusion of embryos, and technological manipulation beyond those allowable under lawful boundaries." David read from the charge sheet before him. The list was extensive, so he and Jonah had agreed that he'd work on the prosecution of the warrior program and offences against the government while others would focus on other aspects, including the financial practices of Marylou and her cohorts.

Marylou stared at him.

"Fine, we have enough evidence to prove the charges, Marylou. If you happen to have any extenuating circumstances, we'd be more than happy to hear them."

She sat there, resolute, and David knew any further discussion would be pointless.

"Fine. We know that you are not the apex of this organization, but you have infused some fifty-seven million credits in the last year to the cause. You organized, retrofitted, and allowed the building of a base within the World Bank, outside the terms and conditions of your position. You also funneled at least fifteen percent of all unallocated funds the bank earned into the cause."

Her eyes darted left and right, as if waiting for someone to enter and save her. Her lips were a thin, white line as her fingers clutched convulsively at the small necklace she wore.

David stood and made his way around to her, settling on the edge of the desk. "Look, Marylou, I want to help you, but you're going to have to give us something if you want us to cut you a break."

Now a smile split her face, feral as she moved, fingers twisting the necklace. She aimed the tiny, sharp implement at him, but he was trained to move quickly, so shoving off the table, he captured her wrist, twisted, and when she squeaked the item dropped to the floor. He kicked it away with a *tsking* sound.

"Fine, we'll take that as you have nothing left to say."

Jonah had sat through the short meeting then rose. "Guards!"

They entered, cuffed the woman, and lifted her as she started to scream at them, swearing and threatening their annihilation as she was led from the room.

David bent and retrieved the dart, taking great care to avoid the tip, and slid it into a small bag for Michael to test later.

David turned to Jonah. "Better organize to bring in the other one."

They'd checked his identity with his identity chips, and the name that flicked up left him surprised: Carlos Phenja, a young financier and reasonably new to the World Bank.

He was marched in between two guards, his face set into a sneering mask.

David had decided on a different approach with this youngster, uncomfortably aware that something was off. He'd invited Dr. Aros, the psychiatrist who'd joined the multi-disciplined team they'd assembled, to sit in on the interrogation.

Once the man was settled, David scooped up the desktop scanner attached to the table, checked his fingerprints, and frowned as the system glitched on application. The reading flashing up: *Identity Confirmed. Subject Deceased. Override Required.*

Alarm flashed through him. It had never done that before.

A nod to Jonah and he rose and opened the door, admitting Michael and Dr. Aros. They settled into their seats, and without a word, David handed Aros the scanner screen. His brother frowned at the error messaged displayed on the screen.

"Let's run a DNA scan then."

At Michael's comment, the young man's eyes widened in alarm. *Definitely something odd here.*

"*No!*" Layers of panic settled on their subject's face, betrayed that there was something to find.

Michael rose, reaching into his pocket for his small medi-scanner, and the Phenja tried to rear away.

David moved around the table, anchoring Phenja as he fought Michael, shoulders twisting, body bucking.

Michael swore as the man bounced, catching him under the jaw. "Dammit, I'll tranq you if necessary." He shoved the reader into his arm, the input syringe darting out and capturing a sample, which he then connected to the desk scanner unit.

Error messages flared on the screen. "DNA incompatible. What the fuck is going on?" Michael bent and entered a short sequence before sucking in a deep breath, the action

catching David by surprise as much as the draining of color from his brother's face. "You're Carlos Phenja?"

The youngster stared at Michael, no smile. No way to decode whatever emotions were rolling around inside him.

David stepped around to read the screen. "Subject deceased. What the hell?" Michael pierced Phenja. "He's dead. So, who are you?"

The smile on Phenja's face, cold and malicious, stopped David's heart for an instant.

"Someone you wish you'd never found."

The lightning change in the personality confused as much as terrified David. This wasn't a straightforward form of evil, it was a new and infinitely dangerous kind.

He pressed the communicator button connected to the guards outside the door. "Call for Dr. Windhower. She might be able to shed some light on what's happening."

They waited in silence, minutes passing, each taking on the effect of an hour, leaving them time to consider individually the variety of reasons for the anomaly.

A knock came at the door. David called out, "Enter!"

Sara, his brother's friend and a specialist medic, slid through the partially open door.

"You called for me?" She cast her glance around the room then blinked rapidly upon seeing the young man before her. "I know you, don't I?" Her brow furrowed as she pointed a finger at Phenja, and David's confusion grew.

"We have a problem with ID. It reads as deceased." His bald statement led to her mouth opening in an 'O.'

"Let me see." She hurried to the scanned. "Oh no! Who? Who did this? Was it Colvert or one of his cronies?" Fury etched every syllable of her speech and the youngster, Phenja, simply smiled.

"What?" Jonah groused, and Sara turned to their superior.

"I know this patient, because he was presented as a candidate for cybe-therapy. I couldn't allow it as he had a degenerative disease. Let me check my files, to be sure." She reached into her pocket and withdrew a tiny tablet device. She tapped, stopped, then added more information. "A degenerative cognitive disease making him an unsuitable candidate. The family wanted to offer inducements, which I could not allow. I made arrangements for palliative care and sent him home. Or at least the person whose body you inhabit, wasn't it? Because you couldn't have survived with that poor prognosis for more than eight weeks. That was maybe eighteen months ago."

Sara advanced, swept aside Phenja's hair, and sucked in a deep breath, then beckoned to David. Now that they knew what they were looking for, it was easy to find the tell-tale cues. Stitch marks, still an angry red, circled his head under the hairline, and David had to gulp down the wave of nausea threatening to swamp him.

What are we dealing with? But the truth, as fantastical as it seemed, was there. Surgery. His throat narrowed, and speaking posed a problem. "A transplant?"

Sara turned back to the assembled team. "Brain transplant. I'd read about it. It would be right up there with the work of Colvert and his predilection for trying new and *avant-garde* procedures."

CHAPTER TWENTY

*E*rin had just organized delivery of a meal direct to her apartment when the knocking started on her door.

Tottering to the door, the roar of David's voice left her wondering what she'd done now. His voice sounded imperiously. "Open this door or by heaven's I'll break it down."

"Okay, I'm coming!" Her hand turned the old-fashioned knob even as she frowned. As the door opened, David was pushing in, past her to turn and face her near the opening to her bathroom.

"What have I done now?" The quiver of her voice betrayed her emotions.

"What are you doing here? Get your stuff now." He glared, and she squared her shoulders, trying to sort through the tangles of his furious demand.

"What do you mean? This is my accommodation and—"

He reached out and pulled her against his rigid body. "You're coming with me, back to my place. That's where you belong."

Her harsh laugh echoed. "Oh, that's rich! After what you said to me? There's no way in hell I'm going to do that. You apologized. I accepted, but that doesn't give you the right to assume I'll come back for more of your type of caring. I don't want or need that." Her chest bellowed with the force of getting the words out.

Of all the asinine assumptions someone could make!

He dropped his hands, his gaze roaming her face. "Erin, we talked about—"

"You apologized, sure. But we didn't agree to continue this..." she sputtered. Flinging her hands into the air, she leaned in. "Because I don't know what the hell it even is! You hurt me. You dismissed me, and now you want to take up again? Over my dead body. I'm not a toy you can have then get sick of. I told you, being alone is safer, and you reinforced it with your attitude."

David stumbled to the bed, dropped down, and covered his eyes with shaking hands. "I need you to understand, Erin. This thing between us is vital to me. To us. I was wrong, and yes, I know I hurt you." He dropped his hands, pleading with his eyes.

"You don't have to—"

"I do, Erin. You're right. You're not a toy, and you did tell me. I lost myself in what I remembered and allowed it to cloud my judgement. What I did was unforgivable. I don't know how..." He swallowed, his adam's apple bobbing in his neck.

Erin whirled away, the sight too much. He'd done wrong, but she couldn't bear to see the pressures and stress he was dealing with. She wasn't an unfeeling woman, and his despair on top of her own was too much.

Tears sprang to her eyes, burning. God, how she wanted to believe that he wouldn't hurt her again.

Her psyche screamed that she didn't need a man, but her soft heart whispered of hope and companionship. Of love.

"David, I..." *How do I take a leap of faith and still protect myself?* It was a question with no answer. Instead, she stepped closer. "I want to believe you. But I don't know how."

"I know." He looked so defeated, shoulders rounded, and he slumped before her. "I didn't think about what I was saying. I lashed out. Irrational, yes, but also thoughtless."

The gulf between them seemed both small and yet so great. She reached out, in that instant realizing she had to make an effort, because she'd eternally regret it if she didn't.

His fingers curled around hers, warmth seeping into her chilled flesh.

"Come with me." He spoke so quietly she strained to hear. As his words filled her mind, the temptation beckoned.

"Not yet, David. Give me time. I need to think, and I guess work out whether I can give in. What I feel is so jumbled. I was sure until this, but it's unfair to lump you with all the blame. I should know, and I don't. Until then, it's not fair to either of us. But I want to find out, with your help."

David's lips curled into a grimace. "I guess that's fair. More than fair. But give me a chance, Erin. Give us a chance."

Her nod was tight as she agreed.

Now she moved away. "I've ordered a meal for here, would you like me to arrange one for you?" If she agreed to give them a chance, then the opportunity to talk without others and interruptions seemed the first step.

"So long as you're okay with that, then I'd appreciate it."

With shaking fingers, she communicated with the mess, increasing the meal order to enough for two, then she turned back. "Your interrogation?"

This time, as he closed his eyes, she felt a jolt.

"What's wrong?"

"Multiple layers of wrongness, Erin. They've been working on transplants." He shook his head. "Some things should never be tinkered with."

Confused, she wrinkled her brow. "They've been doing those for centuries. What could they have—"

"Brain transplants."

"*What?*" Containing her screech was impossible as she stared. "What the hell are you talking about? That's a class five breach of the transplantation ruling!"

"Yeah. Phenja is the first we've found, but I'm not going to say I won't be surprised if we find others. Windhower—the doc who operated on Michael—she made the discovery when we couldn't make an ID match. The machines glitched, and it seems she had been called in to make a determination on a patient almost two years ago. He had some kind of degeneration of the brain and passed. They used the body, and no one quite knows how, where, or whom at this point. I've got Senna and Fairburn out with Franklin, tracking down the patient's family. Hoping to connect so we can find out who and where."

"The more we dig, the worse it is. But never in my wildest dreams would I have expected this." She really hadn't. On uncertain legs, she tottered to the bed and sank down. "Brain transplants. You think Colvert is the culprit?"

"I don't know, honestly. He was involved with Clarissa's situation twelve to eighteen months ago, and I wouldn't be surprised if his nose isn't somewhere in this mess. But that's not all. I think their first group of IVF successes have matured far enough for them to impregnate them. I came across a girl in a lab. They were in the process of implanting a viable embryo."

Generation Two. She knew what that meant. Those babies would be enhanced, and the cycle would be harder to break. The problems with those children were worse than the generation before, as they grew up without emotion.

"We have to stop them."

"We're closer than before. Marylou and Phenja are in custody. We're tracking Sorrington and should have him soon. Some of the biggest financial backers have been apprehended, cutting off their supply line. We're hurting them. We've got one of their biggest doctors, and we know who the political puppets are. Once we get the lynchpin, we can start to shut down the pyramid." A knock at the door echoed, and she glanced in its direction. David rose and headed for the door. "Hopefully that's dinner."

It was, but what could and should have been a companionable dinner became instead yet another strategy session as they considered what they knew, what they needed to know, and filled in the gaps as best as possible.

D avid woke early, glaring at the ceiling. It was a mess, and he didn't just mean the shambles he'd made of his life.

A brain transplant would need theatres, specialists, including anesthetists and teams. Who had carried it out? Where was there a facility big enough where no one would question what was happening?

It had to be a remote location.

It didn't even have to be this continent, but a city big enough where the anonymity wouldn't raise eyebrows. But nothing came to mind, and he seethed at his inability to see clearly and work out the where of it all.

Throwing aside his covers, he rose up, and it hit him like a ton of bricks. "The bloody bank! They had operating theatres, and people come and go all the time, so no one would raise an eye. I was in the bloody room and didn't even connect the dots!"

Excitement fizzed through his nervous system as he tugged on clothing, then he stopped. They could be wrong. To be sure, he'd need a multi-disciplinary team to investigate what was possible. He'd need Michael, Erin, and some other guards so they could hunt through the building. The biggest problem he could see would be that they'd come back and— *Bzzt!* The blare of his communicator captured his attention, and he glanced down. "Shit!"

One of his informants had sent him a text. The children were converging on the bank. He had to get there before they did.

Grabbing the ignition device for the vehicle, he demanded the device to contact Michael, Sevres, Fairburn, and Erin, requesting their immediate attendance.

He stopped outside Erin's block in time to see her hurry down the steps. He flung open the door, and she dove inside. They took off, asphalt flying as he accelerated. The guards at the gate saw him coming and raised the gate just in time. He screamed onto the road, the car almost floating above the ground as he tried to beat them to the location.

Gaining ground, his gaze set on the road before him, he pushed the vehicle beyond the specifications, hyper-aware of the woman beside him. "They're converging on the bank, and I bet that's where they were undertaking the transplantation. They'll be looking to remove the traces before we can find the information we need."

Erin reached out, touching his hand. "We could be too late. Michael and Clarissa both said you'd gathered medical data, maybe that's all we need to prove what they're doing. It's okay if we don't get there though. We've got Phenja, and he's proof enough."

David's brain registered her words, tossing them over. Considering the facts as she presented them. The tension that had wound inside him now released, washing away, leaving him strangely comfortable with her statement.

He'd collected all the medical data they'd found, confiscating their medi-comp units. Slowing the car, he pulled into a street near the building, opening communications with the others who were leaving the base. "Belay my command. The children are there, and McNally and I are in location, watching. We're too late for the building, but the information is probably already on hand."

The street filled as dozens and dozens of children converged, civilians watching from the comparative safety of their buildings, curtains twitching at windows. For the first time, he saw something akin to fear crossing people's faces as they peered out. Those who'd been in the streets when the children converged huddled in doorways, banging on them and seeking entrance, looking for somewhere to hide from the human mass.

The first bang rippled through the air, those crouching outside slinging hands over their heads and ducking down.

Louder came the explosions, and Erin's hand snaked across the console, burrowing inside his grasp. "They must have worked out what we would be looking for. They may not yet know that we've got the computers. It's not great. I know you wanted videographic evidence, but what we have is a start, David. It's more than we had before, and no one else made the connection."

It wasn't nearly enough to his thinking, but Erin was talking sense.

He could take on the blame for missing these facts, or focus the information they'd gleaned They just needed to wade through it.

"We can put the professor and Windhower onto going through what we have."

Erin nodded. "They'll find what we need and quicker than anyone else. We just need to use our resources wisely."

The building came crashing down at four thirty-seven in the morning as they watched. The ripple through the financial world would only be second to the loss to their investigations he thought. Slowly, the children dispersed, and they watched as they moved away, expressions calm and relaxed, apparently unconcerned at what they'd done.

Only when David was sure it was safe did they head back to the base, in silence.

Erin contacted the others and had them meet at the laboratory for an update, that having become the unofficial office for the mission.

Everyone clustered within as he and Erin shared what they'd seen, what he'd worked out. From there they had to hand out follow-up tasks. Professor Venos and Sara Windhower working their way through the reports and charts they'd retrieved when they'd cleared the building. Franklin and Senna, together with Fairburn and Sevres, would begin searching in earnest for Sorrington, while he and Erin would continue the interrogation of Phenja and Gantry.

"Once we have the information, the senator and Jonah will begin a campaign of media releases. We've already got the vision of the gestation chambers and children, and once we place Phenja and Gantry on trial, that too will be televised. We need to get as much information out there as we can. The people are scared now. The loss of the World Bank was a wake-up call for all the citizens locally."

Erin stood beside him. "We saw them just as the populace did. Until now, the only other major loss that impacted on them was the hospital and babies. Until now, we've never had any kind of evidence to show the populace. We need to use this, in the most effective fashion. The people need to know that if the children take over the political arm, any form of government will crumble. That's what we need them to know."

The team dispersed, leaving David and Erin standing there, beside the whiteboard he'd used to create his web of information. "We can win this war, Erin."

"Are you trying to talk yourself into believing that?" She smiled, and he sucked in a deep breath.

"I don't know so much about that, but once we have a plan, we can move forward."

"I need a coffee. Join me?" She quirked her brow at him, in an almost coquettish fashion. He wrinkled his brow. "Whatever you want to give me, is what I want." And he meant it.

CHAPTER TWENTY-ONE

*P*henja seemed to have shrunk overnight. Something about
him twigged as familiar while Erin watched the oddities
of his movements. From the way he flicked his hand out dismissively
to when he thought no one was looking the imperious way he tugged
at the restraints. She couldn't put a finger on it, just knew that it
twigged a memory of someone she'd met.

"David, something about Phenja is annoying me."

He cast a sideways glance at her, and she grunted.

"Not like that. I just mean he's got these mannerisms. I don't know
why, but I'm sure I know him from somewhere. It's like I know him,
but the person he is isn't the person I'm thinking of."

Defeat crashed down on her at the inability to call up her memory.
They moved back into the room, settling at the table, and she took the
lead as they'd agreed. "So, Phenja, we know that isn't your name. It's
only a matter of time until we work out who you are, so you could
make our job easier."

He sneered, "But that's not what I plan to do."

"Fine. Let's take a look, shall we? You underwent a brain transplant. Scary stuff that. What if it hadn't worked? Everything you know
would have been lost. That didn't bother you?"

He shrugged, and she moved on, undeterred by his apparent disinterest.

"You have a history, no doubt. One you're probably proud of. Likely in banking or some kind of high-ranking position, given the way Gantry deferred to you. I wonder what that was."

He remained silent, and she decided to try a different tack.

"Okay, so they felt you were important enough to transplant your brain. Your body must have been breaking down or broken. Which was it? You must have been dying—knowing that the end was looming." She leaned over the desk, seizing his attention with her eyes. "Death is such a final act. Were you reliant on a machine to survive? Had your body failed you that much? What was it like, knowing that your final breath was drawing near?"

Erin waited, watching for the blinking of his eyes, seeking any chink in the armor he drew around himself.

"Were there medical specialists and machines beeping incessantly?" She needled, seeking an opening, something to break his total self-absorption. "I'll bet it was unpleasant, right? They were taking care of your bodily functions. Just think, someone else caring for your toileting, must have sucked. Did you have to wear a diaper?"

The sneering grew sharper, and this time he flinched, and while she wouldn't inwardly rejoice, she knew she'd hit the nail on the head.

He'd likely been a proud man, but with a failure of his own abilities to care for himself, it would have galled him to consider having others take on his most intimate care, and perhaps he avoided thinking about it? That would make sense. Ignore it, refuse the truth, and it became nothing more than a figment of his imagination, she thought.

"Of course, then there would have been medications, shots, and sprays that you would have had to take. You probably still need anti-rejection medications monthly, right? I guess at least you're still alive, even if the body they gave you isn't agile. I've seen the way you struggle to move. It's rather graceless."

Phenja bared his teeth. "You know nothing."

"Perhaps I don't have to know everything. *Yet*. Even now, our team is searching through the records we seized." When he jerked, she smiled. "Yes, we did collect everything we could when you were taken. We've already worked out they were using rooms in the bank as the operating theatre. I don't know exactly what they found there, having been somewhat *tied up*."

He growled at her light-hearted words, just as she'd planned for him to. The pressure was working, but she wasn't sure how much longer this would take. They'd already been working with him for three hours. He'd grown paler the more she'd talked. David watched, moral support and interested bystander so far.

David touched a light finger to her hand, and she glanced at him, seeing the unspoken suggestion in his eyes. They rose without a word and headed for the door, but before she followed David from the room, she glanced back, unable to resist a final jibe. "But hey, now it's your turn, right?"

She slipped from the room, and David grinned. "I just got a message from Sara. She thinks they've worked out who Phenja is. She needs us at the lab, but he's—"

"Going to need a break. I don't reckon we'll get much out of him right now. Besides, I've given him a lot to think about. We'll get the guards to escort him to his cell. If you want, the professor or Michael can check him over. He's going to need a bathroom break anyway."

He indicated to the guards, relayed her suggestion, and together they headed for the health center, knowing that whatever Sara had discovered might just give them an insight into who was behind the whole plot.

K nocking on the door, David ushered Erin into the tiny office where Daniella, Jonah, Michael, Clarissa, and Sara had clustered around a small comp-unit. "We got your message."

"Excellent. Now that I have you all here, you're going to want to see what I've found."

They crowded around, and Sara brought up the files. "This is the file for Phenja. As you will clearly see, his degeneration was well advanced when he came to my attention. I would expect this was only weeks before the death of his body, which would be compromised in the long-term should it be allowed through to end of life."

The room remained silent as everyone scanned the information on the screen.

"They would have moved him into an assigned facility, I think, within the bank. Like a clean room where we keep mainframe back-ups. They wouldn't have wanted to compromise his physical health, although from my previous records, he'd been involved in an accident in early childhood, hence the gait. The parents of the donor body wanted cybe-therapy at the suggestion of his attending physician, Albert Larossa—a peer of Colvert from his medical student days."

David knew the name. "No, Larossa was a financier who disappeared just over a year ago, about the time we found Clarissa..." His stomach curdled as something else occurred to him. "Is he Phenja?"

"Albert Larossa had a brother. Gilbert. Much younger, and yes, a financier." Sara nodded in silence while the rest gasped in shocked silence.

"You've been able to prove that beyond a shadow of a doubt?" Jonah demanded.

Sara scrolled through the files. "I've found a range of information, including the operative notes, DNA sampling data, and even more importantly, video footage proving it all. Gilbert Larossa is Phenja—the man we have in custody."

Nausea rolled in David's belly as he considered what they'd done. When he turned to Jonah, his brother-in-law had a bright red face. "They've broken every rule, used people for their own ends. I want details. Everything on him. This can't and won't be disregarded." Jonah's voice vibrated with fury.

They left the building together, Erin trailing behind with David as he churned over what they'd learned. "If they can use bodies like this, then that tells me they have no compunction killing and using indiscriminately."

He grunted as she stopped him, her hand soft on his arm. "David? Do you think that's what they planned to do with Clarissa in the end?

What about me, would they have used me like that if you hadn't found me in time?"

The slow burn of anger that had been fanned with their findings burst to life. "I wouldn't have let them, Erin. You mean too much to me."

Her eyes carried a haunted shadow in their depths. "That's all well and good, David, but we both know if you'd been much longer, it would have been too late for me. I was already hypothermic, according to Michael."

He tugged her close, inhaling the scent of her and letting the warmth of her body settle the jittering panic that thrummed in his blood. Considering what could have been was too much to bear. He needed to focus on what they knew, what they'd achieved. Right now, it had to be enough.

"We'll find these bastards, Erin. They will pay for what they've done, for all the manipulations and the transplants."

He knew she'd continue to toss the consequences over in her head. It would play on her mind for a long time to come, but until they had the apex of the group who'd committed the atrocities, and the wound would continue to fester. He'd do everything in his power to stop them, but for now, she just needed his support to deal with the emotional injuries they'd wrought upon her.

Gathering her close, David didn't care who saw them. His heart melted as she leaned into him, accepting the unspoken care he lavished on her.

"I was scared, David. I knew I'd done the right thing, but..." Her hiccup had his eyes closing as his heart squeezed.

Erin always exhibited a strong front, yet here she was lost and more uncertain than he'd ever seen her.

Even after the shooting, she'd bounced back full of fire and chutz-pah, but this time seemed to have diminished her fire.

He dragged in an unsteady breath. "Erin, I'm not sure how much longer we can keep up this dance—"

She frowned at him and opened her mouth, but he raised his hand, stopping her before she could speak.

"I know now isn't the time to talk about it, but I have to tell you, that to me, you are everything."

Her eyes shimmered.

"Tonight, I want to talk to you. I mean..." Flustered now, David had to fight to hold onto his wits. This was much harder than he'd imagined. "Look, we'll talk tonight, over dinner. Right now, we need to go see Sara. See what she's found. Then I vote we go hit Phenja with everything we have."

He reached for and grabbed her hand, propelling her toward Sara's office.

He'd just clenched it when an alarm sounded. Anger and frustration welled. His communicator squarked, and he hammered the button. "What?"

"It's Phenja, sir. He's taken something and he's..."

He and Erin turned and sprinted for the hallway even as he demanded a status update. Reaching Phenja's cell took only a minute, but his heart thudded like a rock into his belly. There on the bed lay what was left of Phenja, foam gathering in the spittle around his mouth, eyes open but fixed in a death stare David knew all too well.

"God dammit!" David gave way to the rage at yet another loss.

"He died hard, David. Couldn't face what he knew would come." Erin's words echoed in the silence after she shooed away the guards. They weren't needed now. "He died and took the easy way out. That must have really pissed him off. He had gone to such lengths to avoid it, yet at the end of the day, he embraced death so he wouldn't face justice."

"We need to know what—"

Erin grunted and knelt by the narrow pallet. "It'll be a capsule embedded in a tooth. Some kind of quick-acting poison, probably even if we'd known which, we wouldn't have got an antidote to him in time."

David sighed and pushed away from the wall. "Why do you say that?"

"Because he was still well when we left the interrogation room. If that's the case, I think you'll find he broke the capsule on the way to the cells. The guards wouldn't be watching his face, simply focused on getting him back here and settled." She rose. "We should call Michael to check the body though."

Once more, he hailed his brother, carefully explained the situation, and waited for Michael to appear, shadowed by Jonah who scanned the room, then settled his gaze on David. It felt heavy.

"I want your report so we can find out what went wrong with our systems and surveillance."

Obviously dismissed, he and Erin left the tiny room.

CHAPTER TWENTY-TWO

*D*usk settled like a dark blue cloak, the air releasing from the tropical tones to a more comfortable temperature. Erin settled into the seat at the tiny table in the Officer's Club to wait for David. He'd contacted her, stating the time and the location, much to her consternation.

Erin wasn't sure she was up for much discussion of their failures tonight, given she still struggled with the truth of how close she'd come to dying.

The door jangled, and Erin looked up. She watched as David sauntered to the bar, ordered, then waited for the drink. Then, with a quiet word to the bartender, he wound his way through the empty tables to where she sat, waiting.

The scrape of the chair on the scarred wood flooring was an insult to her ears.

"You don't look very happy," Erin murmured.

He sighed. "I'm not really. I mean, losing Phenja was..." David shook his head. "Look, let's not talk about the case tonight. It's not why I asked you here."

Flags of crimson flared across his cheekbones, and he evaded looking at her.

Instinct welled, and the wine she'd just drunk turned glutinous in her belly, thickening enough to make her feel queasy. *He's going to end this.*

When David reached out, Erin struggled to contain the flinch that was instinctive.

All good things must come to an end. Even the bad ones.

He gulped, and her mouth turned dry.

"Erin, I want to tell you that these last weeks have been both a heaven and a hell to me."

He inhaled deeply, nostrils flaring as if he were mentally girding himself.

"David, don't feel that you have to..." The words were so hard to push out. How to tell him that she understood? That although they tore her apart piece by piece, she'd accept that and move along. Her mouth was dry, and she shied away from looking at him.

When he cleared his throat, she was sure the tears welling in her eyes would give away her sudden inner turmoil.

He looked her in the eyes, frowned, and reached out. "What? No! You think I'm bringing this to an end?" The incredulity in his voice echoed in the still room. "That's not what I was trying to say. I've gone about this in a ham-fisted manner, sure, but not calling this to an end. Dammit! Erin, I want to marry you."

The words exploded into her brain, searing her neurons, and her chest swelled, leaving her unable to breathe, so she simply stared at him for a moment. His gaze narrowed, and Erin realized he needed her to respond. Thoughts took a moment to gather, and all that squeaked out was, "Marry me?"

"Yes. Dammit, when they took you, I nearly went mad. I would have ripped the place apart by myself, but Jonah stopped me. That was when I really understood that I couldn't live without you. That you weren't just important to me, but vital to my ability to think, to be. Erin, if you're not ready or need more time—"

She grinned, then shot up, reached for him, and grabbed his shoulders, suddenly sure. "I don't need more time."

Erin tugged, grateful when he stood up so she could kiss him, her lips firm against his, trying to tell him with her whole being that it didn't just overwhelm her, but also filled her with joy.

The sound of a clearing throat broke through the veil of sensuality that sparked around them.

Releasing David took far more effort than simply letting go. Her gaze meshed with his, and the slow grin married with the twinkle in his eyes had her stomach lurching.

"I'm still waiting for an answer." He spoke roughly, as if unsure and hopeful in equal turns.

"I, uh..." She cleared her throat, aware suddenly of other eyes settling on her, heavy with interest. "Do we have to do this here?"

He laughed. "Yes."

Closing her eyes, Erin sought the inner peace, waited a second as she inhaled and pushed away everything unimportant. The only thing that mattered in the here and now was David, the question he'd asked, and her feelings.

"Yes, David. I will marry you."

"Good. Then let's make it official, shall we?" He reached into his pocket and withdrew a dark blue, velvet pouch. "This was my grand-mother's. I want you to wear it."

The ring he tugged out was old, set with diamonds and sapphires. Not large and flashy, but modest, with the stones deeply set in a gold band.

With shaking fingers, she accepted the ring on her left hand. It might be whimsical, but Erin was sure there was something about the ring that emanated security, happiness, and hope.

Once he'd slid the ring onto her finger—and it fit perfectly—he took her hand and cleared his throat. "Let's get out of here."

Erin stood, leaving her half-finished wine on the table, and followed him from the Officer's Club. Right now, destiny was painting her future, and she couldn't wait to see it.

David slid his arm around Erin, aware that the few gathered in the Officer's Club would be sharing the tale far and wide. He didn't care, because he'd got his Erin, finally.

"I asked the others to wait for us," he said.

"The others?" she asked.

"Michael and Clarissa, Jonah and Daniella. They knew what I planned and are waiting to hear the outcome. They're at Jonah's office, and I'd like to share our news. Is there anyone you want to contact?"

Erin shook her head. "No. Everybody who's important to me is here, on the base."

They trudged forward, to the office where the others waited, but he savored the quiet time, all too aware that the final push would be coming soon, and things would once more become frantic and dangerous.

At the door, Erin stopped. "I'm uh... What if they think I'm not the right one?"

The anxiety in her voice stopped him, made him frown. "They don't think that at all. In fact, they've known since the incident with Daniella that I've been gone on you. They all respect and like you. What's more, I know they're going to be ecstatic that you said yes."

Without giving her time to re-think, he ushered her inside, where everyone waited in silence. He nodded, Jonah hooted, and Michael slapped his thigh. Daniella and Clarissa descended on Erin with hugs and 'welcome to the family' comments.

The fingers of dawn slid across the walls as Erin lay nestled in David's arms. The ring, a new and somewhat disconcerting addition, weighed on her finger. He'd asked for a date, and she'd suggested waiting a week or two. He'd argued that there was no need to wait, and she'd caved. In two weeks, they'd make their vows— unless something else happened.

Before she could consider any kind of preparation though, she needed to know more about Phenja. To wrap up the whole situation in a be-ribboned bow. Who was he?

She'd met him somewhere, Erin was sure of that. Sara had said he was Gilbert Larossa, but she'd never met him, although she'd known of his reputation. As a financier he'd been legendary until his apparent suicide. Erin bit her lip, conjuring up a view of him from what she'd seen of his identi-view. Tall and spare-framed with piercing blue eyes.

Those eyes.

"Oh my God!" She bolted up in the bed. "I know who Phenja is. He's Larossa, but he's also Dreck, the underworld figure. They're the same."

She reached for David to wake him, but he was already sputtering to awareness. "What's wrong?"

"I've worked out who Phenja and Larossa are, or were. He died right? Or disappeared and everyone thought he'd committed suicide. He hadn't. He'd just gone underground as Cornelius Dreck, the frail but incredibly dangerous head of the largest underworld movement. He changed his features, jawline and hair color, but he couldn't change his eyes. They were weirdly—"

"Intense. Yes. *Dammit.* As Dreck he'd have contacts through every layer of the underworld. In his other persona, he'd have connections. Lots of connections. He's the uncle of—"

"Lilly Montaine, who is involved with Sorrington. Connections and relatives. It's there just beyond our reach, David. Why can't we see it?"

Erin rubbed her eyes, suddenly aware that time was rolling on and the longer the operation stalled, the greater the risks their adversary would go to ground.

"We need to find the connection," she said. "We know Phenja wasn't the one in charge, though he called the shots for Gantry, and I'm guessing his position was incredibly powerful. We'll need to make enquiries on that, but I figure he's one of the top honchos. He's higher up the food chain than any of us previously considered, David, and I think we've come across the person in charge already in our investigations, because capturing him was far too easy. I think they gave him up, and he accepted that for the greater good of their cause. He was prepared with the poison cap on his tooth. He knew we would break him, so he ended it before he could spill anything important." Rubbing her hands through her hair, she considered what they'd already put together and made another leap. "It's someone who's well-hidden. Someone with connections."

David pulled her close. "Then if you're right, this is about to blow up. Let's not wait. We get married tomorrow, take today to start our investigations, then..."

It wasn't romantic as far as protestations went, but it was in keeping with their personalities. Erin took a moment, testing her feelings over the matter of rushing their wedding before nodding. "Okay. I need to get the team rounded up, so you organize the official stuff."

Erin tugged back the bedding and rose, heading for the cupboard.

"Are you forgetting something?"

She stopped and turned to look at him, his gaze roaming over her naked form. "What?"

"You'll need a dress."

She stared at him. "A dress?"

"Yes. Unless you're prepared to let me organize that too."

His grin was wicked, and she frowned.

"Maybe." Turning back to the wardrobe, she tugged out the clothes she'd placed in there just yesterday. There wasn't time for her to consider that it felt right, or that there'd been no real sense of disorientation in taking this step of sharing a room or a bed.

Tugging on her uniform, she caught sight of the glint of the ring as she fastened the buttons.

The promises they'd both made. Those yet to come.

It calmed the desperately churning sea that existed inside her. She scooped up her hair, attended to the necessary ablutions, then with a hard, hot kiss, she took her leave of David.

Jogging down the path, she tossed over what she knew of the situation. Phenja and Sorrington, Montaine and—"

She stopped. *Montaine.* Who had the resources? The connections?

Who could sail under the radar without them settling on them? She recalled David and Celeste's chatter about who they knew. Who was the one person with the connections? The ability to prepare and organize? To mobilize?

"No." She started running now, skidding into the rooms they'd taken in the hospital. Reaching the small center, she dashed inside and up the hall until she was there, the team already hard at work.

"I need everything you have on Lilly Montaine. Where she went to school, her background, what she studied, academic results. Don't leave anything out."

In desperation, Erin hunted out her notepad and began scrolling through the notes she'd taken at Celeste's bedside. Lilly Montaine. Academic record and subsequent removal from college. "Why, Lilly? What did you do?"

Erin rested her fingers on the keyboard, formulating the search string she'd employ. With care, she typed in *Lilly Montaine Ivy League College* and hit the enter key.

In her mind, she was sure the search took hours to conclude, then hits flashed on the screen. One after the other. Her successful entry to Entervale College, the social activities she'd participated in, as well as stories about the politically motivated student and her connection to the new *Citizens Justice Party*.

"That's dangerous company you were keeping," breathed Erin.

It had all been there, right under her nose.

The computer beeped as information was sent to Erin by the team, information on Lilly's expulsion from Entervale Private College, the rapid climb to the head of the politically dangerous party on campus. Her wild parties on returning home, and frequent absences.

The team pulled every scrap of information, while Erin interviewed Celeste one more time, then she sat down to formulate her report and prepare her plan to capture the woman at the heart of the political wasteland that had become their planet.

David wafted in mid-morning and interrupted her, sliding some paperwork in her direction. "Fill these out now and tomorrow we can get married."

Erin didn't scan the paperwork, simply scrawled her name then turned back to her work. Her focus on her work all-encompassing, she didn't realize how long she'd been at it until her team stood and turned off their computers..

"Come on, Erin. Time to go home." Fairburn strode up to her and reached down, lifting her away from the terminal.

She glanced at him owlishly. "What?"

"The day is over, Erin. Time to go home." Sevres took her by the arm. "It's late. We've worked and got as much information as we can. There's nothing more we could do tonight." Sevres walked her to the door, then barred her entry back into the tiny work area as she tried to retreat. "Go home."

"But—"

Beside her, out of the shadows, emerged David. He took her hand. "Time to go home."

The touch of his hand melted her remonstrations, as did the flare of heat in his eyes. Without a word, she followed him from the hospital.

CHAPTER TWENTY-THREE

*D*avid couldn't understand how Erin had become so downright integral to his peace of mind. Tonight, she'd stay with Jonah and Daniella, and he wasn't sure how that made him feel— well, except for lonely and restless. Sleeping without her beside him didn't seem right.

He shifted in the bed, plumping the pillow and missing the warmth of her body next to him.

Tomorrow was the first day of their forever, but tonight he had time to think over what had happened. He groaned and glanced in the direction of the window. Weariness dragged at him, the night passing slowly. The clock on the bedside table glowed green in the darkness. Three fifty-nine. Another seven hours and one minute before she'd meet him in the middle of the training area.

He closed his eyes and groaned, once more wishing for her company, her soft laugh.

Cracking his eyes open again, he peered at the clock and sighed. Four AM... Seven hours.

The night had passed in a strange fashion. Daniella and Clarissa had both settled in for the evening, while the men had caroused before they must have bunked in with David. Sometime around eleven the women had hunkered down in the lounge room, telling Erin it was *time to sleep*.

"Brides with bags under their eyes are very unattractive," added Daniella.

In the morning, Daniella shoved Erin into the bathroom with a coy, "Go shower," which hadn't made any sense until she returned to find a large hanging bag on the door.

The women had made themselves comfortable on the bed.

Clarissa threw Erin a bag and said, "You might want to put these on." Then she indicated that Erin should head back to the bathroom. She opened the bag, and the contents made her blush. Filmy white underwear designed to almost strangle her.

When she entered the bedroom again, both women launched from the bed and circled her.

In the light of morning, the constriction in Erin's chest eased as a tiny seed of excitement cracked.

"Where's the baby?" Erin stared with intent at Clarissa.

"Daddy duty today. I'm all yours. Now, let's get you hooked up, and Daniella is going to attend to your hair."

They fluffed and primped, makeup and hair taking an interminable time, but they refused to let Erin look in any mirror, stating her chance would come later.

Instead, she had to subside, let them have their fun, and wait for their energies to flag. They didn't; not quickly anyway.

Finally, the two women stood back. They smiled and nodded. "Now you're ready to get dressed," said Clarissa.

"Oh, one thing missing," added Daniella, who turned to the tiny bag she'd left on the bed. She tugged on the yellow drawstrings, which matched the satin bag.

When she turned back, Daniella held a chain and from it dangled a sapphire of the darkest blue.

"This was my grandmother's necklace, which David inherited," Daniella said. "He asked me to see if you'd wear it today."

Tears stung Erin's eyes, and she blinked.

"Oh, don't cry." Clarissa rushed forward, thrusting a tissue at her. "You'll ruin your makeup."

"I..." The thickness of her voice didn't surprise Erin. Something about the attention to detail had always been a hallmark of David's actions, and today especially, it held so much meaning. "I'd love to wear it."

Daniella grinned at her and spun Erin around.

The metal settled against her heated skin, cooling and soothing at the same time, and Erin couldn't stop herself from stroking the gem as it nestled in the valley between her breasts.

"Now, stand back so we can get your gown ready for you to step into it." Clarissa reached for the zipper and tugged, the rasp loud to Erin's hearing.

At their direction, Erin stepped into the pool of white satin and lace. "You never said where you found this gown."

Daniella coughed. "It was my mother's wedding dress. She sent it before I married Jonah, but it didn't fit me, and I... It wasn't right for me. She had it made from an antique pattern she found before she married our father and sent it along with a ton of other stuff."

Erin slid a hand over her hips. "Can I look now?"

"Let's get the buttons done up, then yes." Clarissa worked quickly then steered her in the direction of the antique mirror in the corner of the room.

The sight that met Erin's gaze stunned her. It was her, but a very different Erin. This one had sloe eyes, her short hair was fluffed and puffed yet still framed her face, and the makeup wasn't heavy. It merely accentuated what and who she was.

But the gown? It was ethereal. A satin sheath overlaid with delicate lace that flowed over her hips. Her arms, more muscular than Daniella's, were on show with the sleeveless bodice. The gown swished around her ankles yet hugged her body.

"I can't believe this is me." Her breath misted the mirror as the two women crowded behind her.

"It's you. Now, let's get the final touches in place. David will be pacing back and forth until you get down there."

Daniella slid a rose and fern wreath onto her head then thrust a small bouquet of fern and white roses into her hands. "These came from the captain's garden, and Clarissa arranged them last night."

Erin's hands shook, and she slid a last glance at herself then turned. "Let's go."

They walked without hurry out the door of the small house, the women beside her, sisters of her heart, hooking their arms through hers. They made their way across the asphalt to the training yard that had been decorated for the event, according to Clarissa.

A small marquee stood in the middle, and troops loitered, watching with interest, Erin surmised, as she began the slow walk toward David. He wore his dress uniform of dark green, the shine of buttons and medals, his gloved hands neatly folded by his sides, but in the sunlight his eyes glinted. She knew the instant he recognized the jewel, a big, slow smile spreading over his face.

In that instant, the need to run to him burgeoned, and it took willpower and the steadying influence of the two women walking by her side to keep her steps slow and measured.

He could tell; she knew by the way the crinkles beside his eyes scrunched up, his smile widening to a grin. *Dammit!*

David extended a hand in her direction, and the love in his gaze filled her heart with joy so it beat faster and warmed every infinitesimal part of her body.

When she reached David, he took her hand, squeezed. "You're here and look ravishing."

Laughter bubbled in her throat as together they faced Jonah. Ready to embrace the future. "There's nowhere else I'd rather be."

Did you enjoy this book by Imogene Nix?

Feel free to leave a review on the site of your choice and keep reading to find lots of other books by this author!

INHERITANCE OF THE BLOOD BY IMOGENE NIX

In the darkness evil waits...

As a young bride Kira was whisked away from everything and everyone she knew, including her new husband and became Christina, an operative of the Displaced Persons Unit.

As the danger grows she sees an opportunity to save her husband Vasya and sister Serina. But nothing is the same. Serina is grown up—married and pregnant.

Vasya too is older and darkly forbidding. Trusting Christina doesn't come easily until a catastrophic event takes place. Now, knowing the truth everything he thought he knew is changed. But at a very high cost.

The four must work together to defeat the Demon, Zuor and the stakes are higher than they imagined and all could be lost.

The burning at the back of her neck warned she was being watched. A quick glance didn't clarify it. Instead, she turned around in time to see her mother's face, pale. "Mama?"

She took a step forward, but her grandfather snatched her wrist.

The grip was painful, and Kira stilled. "Let your parents talk."

She didn't know what the topic of conversation was, but it couldn't be good.

The dappled sunlight seemed cooler than before.

Her father crooked his forefinger at her grandfather while they stood there. For a moment she wished Vasya had come with them, but he had to work. Just the thought of her new husband warmed Kira.

She only had a few minutes to contemplate her newly defined status as a married woman, when her grandfather pulled at her hand. "Come with me." He tugged and, confused, Kira allowed herself to be towed away.

A glance at her parents' faces stole any feeling of well-being.

"Grandfather?"

"Shh, my love. You must go." His grip was implacable and his face stern, but he shivered.

"What are you doing? Where are you taking me, Grandfather?"

They moved rapidly through the village they'd visited to sell their wares just that morning, and for the first time since they'd arrived in the market place she felt fear. What was wrong? Was it something to do with Vasya?

"You are in danger. We must send you away." The words confused her further. Send her away? Danger?

"Where is Vasya?" She stumbled over a stone, but he kept tugging her onwards.

With a quick glance around, he hauled her into a dirty laneway between the buildings. Kira gasped, trying to drag air into her starving lungs. "There's no time. We must get you away."

A nondescript shopfront lay ahead, and he pushed on the door. It rattled and opened with a loud groan. "Andre? Andre, are you here?"

An older man shuffled into the room, bent nearly double from the weight of the load on his back. "Marat? What do you want?"

"My granddaughter. They are coming for her and us. Get her away. Take her now, while you can."

The man's face clouded over. "Are you sure?"

"Grandfather, where is Vasya?" Fright had the blood in her veins pounding.

"Hush, my precious. Andre will see you well." He turned. "Whatever it takes, Andre. Take her now." With surprising speed, her grandfather whirled and was gone.

The man, Andre, eyed her. "Come this way, child. There is no time to be lost."

Eleven years later

The tattoo of her heart and cry of terror woke her, as they usually did. Once again, as she had since that rapid flight from those who sought her, she found herself in a lonely bed. Hundreds of miles away from everything she'd dreamed of, in a house she'd built for them to share. As always, it left her wishing that Vasya had fled with her.

Instead, here she was, exiled without her husband. With a sob, she rolled over and let the tears fall.

Available from Beachwalk Press
books2read.com/IOTB

THE CELTIC CUPID TRILOGY

When Cupid—otherwise known as Diocail— is banished from his home on a remote Scottish Island, he's set a series of tasks by the great god Lugh, who also happens to be his father.

In **Blame The Wine**, he must bring two lovers together... BBW Cara and James, the man she's lusted over from afar who happens to be a super geek and head Veha Industries.

In **A Stranger's Embrace**, Diocail is driven to help an emotionally fragile Jane and Davis, a famous author. The task is more complicated, with the existence of Carstairs her could-be ex-husband and teenage daughter, Frannie.

In **Revenge on Cupid**, Diocail must take the ultimate chance and find his own happily ever after with Simone. Sometimes the past gets in the way and HEA's don't come cheap though.

The dusty, dingy little diner was full, even with its current state of cleanliness—or lack thereof. People from the surrounding offices didn't care about anything except the incredible, well-prepared food at a reasonable cost. They flooded in, like waves to the shore. As one tide left, another swept in.

"Honestly, Simone. I'm going to try getting his attention one more time. If that doesn't work, I'm out of there. I mean, how long can I keep trying?" Cara picked at the caramel tart she hadn't been able to resist with the cheap metal fork and flicked the blob of fresh cream that sat on top to the side of the plate.

"You've said that tons of times before. Besides, what are you going to do to get his attention? Hmm? Walk naked through the typing pool?" Simone bobbed the straw in her smoothie as she eyed her friend with a frown. "It's been what? Eighteen months since you saw him, and you've mooned over him from a distance ever since you met him. You need to move on, Cara. That is, unless there's something you haven't shared?"

The query was arch. Cara shivered even as she shook her head. "No."

Simone quirked an eyebrow, obviously unconvinced with the answer. Cara let out a deep sigh of frustration. "There's a position...it's only temporary, for a PA reporting directly to him." She speared a forkful of tart, chewed quickly and swallowed, before continuing. "In his office, full-time for the period of the engagement. I saw the memo yesterday. I mean, I have the skills, right? I can type, answer phones, make coffee, file, greet people. What's more, I can probably do it better than all those size eights in the typing pool that Ms. Jackman seems to prefer." She nodded thoughtfully. "All I have to do is get past the ogre in Human Resources."

Simone stared at her, disbelief clear on her face. "Girl, I so remember that woman. If you think you can get past her, you're doing better than I ever did. That's why I left Veha Industries, remember? Maybe it's time to haul out your resumé and consider some other options. Look for something better." Simone shook her head and billows of her crimson hair swirled through the still air.

Cara understood Simone only had her best interests at heart. But this time she knew the outcome would be different. Hell, she could feel it in the air. The tingle of expectation.

"Cara, the HR ogre will hang you out for breakfast before she offers you anything like a position in that office. Remember her mantra? Good looks and good work make for a positive workplace!"

Simone didn't sugar-coat anything. It was another great reason for their long- term friendship. Honesty. But Cara didn't want to hear the truth in the statement. Even if it was exactly as her friend said.

Cara nodded quickly. "Yeah, I know, but if I don't try, then I won't know how close I can get to him, right? And the only way to catch his attention is to get past *her* and see him in person." Cara quaked a little at the information she needed to share. The favor she needed to ask. "Anyway, I tidied up my resumé and dropped the application into a memo envelope yesterday, so it's too late to back out now. I mean, fortune favors the brave. Doesn't it? If I don't snag an interview, I'm going to visit the career advisor across the street and register with them." She shrugged. "I'll look for temp work until something more long-term shows up. I can see what they have on offer and well...who knows? Maybe a job with the right boss is just waiting for me. But I'd rather this worked out, to be honest." Her voice trailed off into a whisper. "I really wish he would notice me."

Simone took a long slurp of her banana drink, and Cara noticed her questioning gaze even as she squirmed. Finally, Simone nodded. "It's your funeral. So anyway, you'd better show me this memo if you want me to be a referee for you. I'm guessing that's what you need, right? I'll have to know what I'm supposed to say about you before they ring."

Cara smiled. "Thanks, Simone. I knew I could count on you." She slipped a piece of paper out of her handbag and handed it over. "Sorry it's a bit creased. It was in the bottom of my bag, I stashed it so none of the others from the pool would see. You know how it is."

Available from Love Books Publishing
books2read.com/CelticCupid

CURSE BOUND

Living in Paradise should be simple...

When Tabitha finally prepares to say her final goodbye to her beloved father, it opens a link to her past and her ancestors. Her inheritance takes her to an island off the Queensland coast, where she discovers she's tasked with finding the answer to the loss of the seafaring ancestor.

Christian, an Archaeologist, enters the scene. Tall, good looking, and interested in Tabitha. When they discover that he's a descendant of the captain's wife, it leaves them both with more questions and danger than they're prepared for.

As they draw closer to finding the key to the long-held secret, it brings many things into question.

Only one is how to defeat the evil incarnate that wants control of what they may find.

My dearest Tabs.

How I wish I wasn't writing this letter. I'd far rather have been there, by your side, when you go home. For home it is. The best home we've ever known.

There is so much to tell you, and yet, how do I even begin?

My sweet daughter, you lit my life from the moment you were laid in my arms.

Everything you did caused me unending delight and pleasure. I don't want to say goodbye, but the doctors have told me honestly, my time is short.

I need to tell you so much!

Our family has a long and proud history of sight...

I stared at the missive. Strangely, it all made sense, while memories long buried in my psyche rose up. Images of my mother, sick with her fingers curled and a look in her eye which frightened me as a child. I gave a tiny shake even now, remembering her eyes. I glanced back down to the paper splotched with salty water that dribbled and dripped. Another tear fell to join those on the lined paper.

I dropped it to the wooden tabletop and sat, numb.

At twenty-three, I was alone.

My hand curled around the glass of wine, and I dashed the tears from my face.

"I'd rather you were here, Daddy. I'd rather you guided me and not left some stupid bit of paper telling me I have to complete some stupid family quest!" I ended on a scream, then dropped my head to the tabletop. "Not even midday and you're talking to yourself. Great start to the next part of your life, Tabs."

There is one task though, something I urge you to take seriously lest you never find your own deep and abiding love. The one I never found. As was the case for my mother and my grandfather. Neither was happy with their choice of partners.

Suddenly, I didn't want the wine. I didn't want the silence of this house. I shoved from the table; the chair overturning and I whirled, ready to hurry from the house when something—someone—stopped me in my tracks. "Who the...?" I couldn't believe the sight before me.

A sad woman, pale and transparent, pinned me with her eyes.

It felt surreal, like I'd walked into some kind of weird television series. "Who are you?" I demanded, the entire time wondering what the hell was going on. Was I hallucinating?

"Michael is lost, as am I. We need you. Only with your assistance can we be free."

I glanced around looking to see if there was some kind of projection, sure at any second, someone would dive out and screech, "You've been punked." I even tried waving my hand through the hologram, but I slid through the image. Nothing shone, and I shivered.

"Are you a ghost?" I felt downright stupid for my comment. My stomach plummeted as the air around me seemed to freeze. "Who are you and what do you want?"

A sad smile flitted over the — and here I hesitated to consider the word — "ghost's" face.

"I am Alice and you must find the Captain. My love, Michael."

The frozen cube of ice that was presently my belly wobbled. "I wouldn't know where to start."

"Finding Michael is the key. Find him and give us both peace." She raised a hand and seemed to fade before my gaze.

"Wait!"

She smiled sadly. *"There isn't much I can tell you, except beware those who will drag you from the path. There are those who will tempt and lie. The very demons of hell."*

"Demons?" I scoffed, and she brushed her hand across her sad eyes.

"You don't remember yet, and this too will dull in your memory, but soon. Someone will come and they will help you see clearly." Then she wavered from view and disappeared.

I shook my head. "No," I told myself and hunted the corners of the room, but the reality slammed hard into me. "I've just had a conversation with a ghost. One who needs my help. Either I need medical care, or I need to find the answers."

Available from Love Books Publishing
books2read.com/CurseBound

Why not subscribe to

Imogene
Nix's
newsletter?

https://www.imogenenix.net/Signup

ALSO BY IMOGENE NIX

Warriors of the Elector

- Star of Ishtar
- Starline
- Starfire
- Star of the Fleet
- Starburst
- The Star of Eternity

The Star of Ishtar & Starline - Print

Starfire & Star of the Fleet - Print

Starburst & The Star of Eternity - Print

Blood Secrets

- The Blood Bride
- The Illuminated Witch
- The Sorcerer's Touch

House Secrets (The Blood Secrets Continuation)

- As Dawn Breaks (Coming in 2021)
- Immortal Consequences (Coming in 2021)

The Automaton Series

- Haven House
- Nobel Crest

The Search Duology

- Miss Elspeth's Desire
- Miss Isabelle's Craving

Reunion Trilogy

- War's End
- The Assassin
- Executing Justice

The Reunion Trilogy in Paperback

The Webs Series

- Tangled Webs
- False Webs (Previously in Sex Love & Aliens Vol 1)
- Covert Webs (Previously in Sex Love & Aliens Vol 2)

21st Testing Protocol

- Cyborg: Redux
- Children Of A Greater Evil
- When Evil Came To Stay (Coming in 2021)
- Finis: The War To End All Wars (Not Yet Released)

Celtic Cupid Trilogy

- Blame The Wine
- A Stranger's Embrace
- Revenge On Cupid

The Celtic Cupid Trilogy in Paperback

Zombieology

- The Reset (2018)— (Love At The End of The World)
- I Dream of Zombies
- The Six Million Dollar Zombie

Knights of Pleasure

- Silken Knights (Not Yet Released)

Single Titles

The Chocolate Affair (also in Print & Audio Book)

Falling In Love Again

BioCybe (also in Print)

Hesparia's Tears (also in Print)

Tomorrow's Promise

A Bar In Paris (also in Print)

Inheritance Of The Blood (also in Print)

The Plan (also in print)

Loving Memories (also in Print)

Hero of Heartbreak Hill (also in Print)

My One & Only

Curse Bound (coming 2021)

Raspberry Dreams (Not Yet Released)

Non Fiction

Self Publishing: Absolute Beginners Guide (With Suzi Love)

Written as Ciara Cave

25 Curated Ways To Get Rid Of Telemarketers

Book Signings for Absolute Beginners

ABOUT THE AUTHOR

Imogene is published in a range of romance genres including Paranormal, Science Fiction and Contemporary. She is mainly published in the UK and USA.

In 2010, Imogene Nix (the pen name not Imogene herself) was born. Imogene sat down and worked tirelessly for 3 months culminating in the book Starline, which became the first in a trilogy titled, "Warriors of the Elector." Since then she's had over 30 titles published and is now focusing on hybridising herself - with a mixture of traditionally published and self-published works.

In fact, she's taking control of many of her back catalogue books, which are slowly re-releasing as self-published titles.

Imogene is a member of a range of professional organisations world wide, and believes in the mantra of mentoring and paying it forward and is actively involved in mentorship (through NaNoWrimo and her vlog: In The Chair With Imogene Nix) and tutoring of new and upcoming authors.

In her spare time she loves to drink coffee, wine & eat chocolate and is parenting her spoiled dog and a ferocious cat along with her husband and 2 human daughters and looks forward to weekends away with her husband in their caravan "The Seven Year Hitch!" Do look forward to her caravan romance at some point!

To Contact Imogene

www.imogenenix.net
imogene@imogenenix.net

facebook.com/ImogeneNix
twitter.com/ImogeneNix
instagram.com/ImogeneNix